AFTERMATH

LISA HARRIS

Adrenaline-Fueled Fiction

Copyright © 2023 by Lisa Harris

All rights reserved.

No part of this book may be reproduced in any form or by any electronic or mechanical means, including information storage and retrieval systems, without written permission from the author, except for the use of brief quotations in a book review.

CHAPTER ONE

"Don't get too comfortable."

Chase Beckett opened his eyes as his brother-in-law, Jace McQuaid, slid into the empty train seat across from him. After ten days of tracking down supplies for the clinic across three cities, he was exhausted and wanted to sleep.

"Trust me, I'm not comfortable," Chase said. "Just dreaming about my queen-sized bed."

And my wife.

The thought made him smile, but just momentarily.

"I understand." Jace glanced toward the door at the end of the train car that was half-filled with passengers. "But actually, I was implying that we might be looking at a bit of trouble."

Great.

He pressed his hands against his thighs and frowned. Two years after the Realm had taken down the grid across the country, there were still organized bands of outlaws emerging from the shadows like cockroaches. And now that the trains were moving again, they'd found a brand new target.

"I ran into an old army buddy of mine who just happens to be the conductor," Jace said, lowering his voice. "There have been rumors of an attack on this route."

Chase glanced out the window of the train, momentarily shifting his focus to the rugged,

west Texas landscape. While this wasn't a pleasure trip, he'd lived through enough excitement over the past two years to last a lifetime. He'd hoped to get home without running into any kind of conflict.

Some had called the attacks on the country by the Realm a second civil war, and he agreed. What he'd seen firsthand had turned into the largest and most destructive conflict on US soil since that era. But just because the good guys had won and the power was finally coming back on didn't mean that the chaos that had erupted across the country had vanished. No. That was going to take time.

Chase rubbed the back of his neck. "It feels like we've just moved from fighting one war to have stepped into another."

"Agreed."

Over the past few weeks, reports had confirmed that there had been hundreds of arrests of all levels inside the Realm, rendering the group powerless. But while law enforcement continued breaking down the corrupt system along with their communication networks, there were those who were still trying to take advantage of the situation.

"What about our supplies and medicine?" Chase asked, turning back to his brother-in-law.

"Nate assures me that they're locked up and there's an armed guard." Jace paused. "But security is spread thin, and he could use the help of any law enforcement on board."

"So you volunteered our services."

Jace grinned. "I know you're tired—"

"I'm fine, though the last ten days have been a bit. . ." Chase searched for the right word.

"Brutal?"

Chase let out a low laugh. "Glad I'm not the only one who feels that way."

He wasn't going to tell his brother-in-law that he was pretty sure he was coming down with something. Instead he'd fight the fatigue like he always did, because there wasn't an alternative. They'd already been gone longer than expected, sourcing supplies from a newly opened pharmaceutical facility for the clinic back in Shadow Ridge. All he wanted to do right now was get back home to his wife.

He reached for his backpack. "All I have to say is that we better not be delayed. I sent our wives a telegram this morning. They're expecting us."

He didn't try to mask the smile the thoughts of his bride brought. If he closed his eyes he could see her full lips, sprinkling of freckles, and soft brown eyes. . .Marrying Hope was the best thing he'd ever done.

But now was not the time to let his thoughts wander.

"I guess we have a job then," he said, standing up. He was determined to get this shipment Hope had requested safely to Shadow Ridge, whatever it took.

Chase slung his backpack across his shoulder and followed Jace through the passenger car toward the front of the train. Two cars down, he caught site of the conductor, a redheaded man in his mid-thirties, wearing jeans, a white shirt and windbreaker, and a cap. A hint of diesel smoke filled the space as he and Jace stepped into the enclosed gangway between the cars, along with the obvious drop in temperature.

"Chase, this is Nate Watts." Jace said, making the introductions.

"It's good to meet you," Nate said, shaking Chase's hand. "Sorry for the noisy location, but I thought this would be the best place for a private conversation."

"Not a problem. It's nice to meet you as well." Chase braced his legs, steadying himself against the rumbling of the train beneath him. "My brother mentioned that the two of you met in the army."

Nate nodded. "The army has always needed reliable transportation, and the rail is—or at least used to be—the most efficient way to move supplies, munitions and even troops."

"And it's becoming essential again," Chase said, "though I bet you never expected to be doing your job while worrying about a train heist."

"Hardly." Nate tugged on his hat. "Jace told me you were involved in taking down the Realm?"

"I was one of many. Worked in Shadow Ridge before the grid went down."

"Seems like an out-of-the-way location."

"It was, but it gave me access without revealing what I was really working on."

"Which was?" Nate asked.

"Security in connection with the McDonald Observatory. We were tracking satellites with a high-speed camera that would record the faint reflections of sunlight. This helped us to track rogue players intent on attacking our space assets."

"So you knew their plan was to take the grid down."

Chase nodded. "I was part of a team helping to provide critical early warning and surveillance of enemy-controlled satellites."

"And yet the Realm succeeded."

Chase nodded, hesitant to relive those dark months, but also not missing the hint of an accusation in the man's voice. Or maybe it was the guilt that still lingered in his own conscience. Before the grid had even gone down, the Realm had managed to logistically prepare for every scenario imaginable, always staying one step ahead. They'd secured dozens of bunkers across the country, heavily stocked with weapons, food, fuel, and water and had created secure communication networks.

Everything they needed to succeed had been implemented into their plan—a plan with an endgame that very few had known about. Exploiting key vulnerabilities had shut down satellites and jammed signals and in turn had hit the country's electric grid, internet, water networks, and transportation system. Because of Chase's security experience, he'd been placed as a mole.

"I spent a few months working in one of their bunkers, trying to take them down from the inside," Chase finally said. "Eventually we were able to do just that."

Nate's jaw tensed. "I knew someone who worked undercover as well. Her name was Rachel Collins."

Chase shifted his stance as the track below them curved, but it was the flood of memories that threw him off balance. The fear in Hope's eyes as Foster had held a gun to her head. Rachel bursting through the doorway and taking the man down. Leading them through a hidden hatch out of the bunker. Rachel taking a bullet that would end her life but ultimately allow him and Hope to escape with the information they'd needed.

It felt just as wrong all these months later as it had back then.

"I knew her," he said finally, trying to gauge Nate's expression, while unsure how much the man knew.

"I know she died in that bunker," Nate rushed on. "We'd planned to get married. . .planned, that is, before the world fell apart."

"She was in the bunker with me," Chase said, wishing there was something he could say to ease the man's pain. "She was working undercover as well, though I didn't know it until the day she died. If it helps at all, she was a true hero. Her job was to keep vital information safe, and she gave her life doing just that."

"That was who Rachel was. Combat medic in the army, medical intelligence, and then undercover." Nate let out a sharp breath. "I always knew she'd give anything for her country. I just wish it hadn't been her life."

"I really am so sorry."

"So am I, but we have our own issues today," Nate said, clasping his hands together. "Sounds like you're both more than qualified to help us out, and we do need help."

"Just tell us how," Jace said.

Nate nodded, the tension still evident on his face. "We're expecting them to hit the baggage area, and they will probably try and stop the train. We're coming up to a section of the tracks where we're going to be forced to slow down, a section where this line has already been hit twice. These outlaws are fearless and, unfortunately, we're understaffed. Most people who would qualify for security jobs with the railroad are already in law enforcement and busy keeping their own towns safe."

"Do you have a plan in place?" Jace asked.

"At this point, we don't know what their strategy is. They could already be inside one of the passenger cars, or they might be planning an ambush when we slow down up ahead. So far, no one has been hurt in any of the heists, but my fear is that passengers could get caught in the crossfire of a shootout, or even hostages taken." Nate drew in a sharp breath. "I'm assuming you're both armed."

Chase nodded and pulled back his wool overcoat revealing his sidearm.

"If you would cover the two front passenger cars, I'd be grateful."

Chase glanced at his brother-in-law then nodded. "Consider it done."

A minute later, Chase headed back to the passenger car where they'd been sitting, while Jace continued on to the next car. His brother-in-law had been right earlier. This trip had been brutal. Between searching for the medicine Hope needed, long hours of travel, and sleeping on the ground most nights, he was ready to be home. The lights might be coming on across the state, but there was still so much that hadn't changed. Lawless towns, gun violence, and the lack of medical care that often meant a simple diagnosis quickly turned deadly.

Chase sat down in the back of the car where he could

see everyone who came in and out. Most were tired after the long journey from Dallas, leaving the train car relatively quiet except for the rumble of the tracks.

He was used to observing people. Watching how they reacted to their environment and to those around them. The man in a baseball cap in the middle of the car stared out the window at the passing scenery. A woman traveling by herself had her hand gripped on her bag, while an older couple across from her sat whispering together. He noted earlier that several of the passengers were carrying sidearms, which made the situation even more dangerous. Especially when he didn't know who the good guys were versus the bad guys.

A woman wearing a red jacket walked into the car, carrying a large bag over her shoulder. He'd noticed her earlier, sitting alone next to a window. She stumbled as the train shook beneath them then grabbed onto the back of one of the seats as her bag slipped off her shoulder.

"Sorry," she said, when the bag bumped into a passenger's shoulder.

The man reached up to shove her bag out of the way, clearly irritated. She stumbled to her seat behind him, but Chase's attention settled on the man who sat facing him. There was something familiar about him. . . A moment later it hit him. Chase had seen the same serpent tattoo on the back of the man's left hand. . .

Elijah Duke.

Chase tugged on his thermal beanie at the realization. Just days before the grid had gone down two years ago, law enforcement from across the entire state had been after both Elijah and his brother Adam, over a long list of charges. They'd tracked them from a south Dallas suburb, west through Abilene, and then all the way to Shadow Ridge where Garrett McQuaid, his father-in-law, had picked up their trail. There had been a showdown near Crowley's Point, where Adam Duke had shot Garrett in the chest.

They'd never found the men, but Chase had no doubt that the brothers were still up to no good.

A second later, Chase smacked his head against the window as the train screeched to a stop. He jumped up from his seat while pulling out his sidearm, but Elijah was already moving toward the exit.

"Elijah Duke," Chase shouted.

Elijah turned around, and in one swift move yanked the woman in the red coat out of her seat and pulled her in front of him. "Sit back down, or I'll shoot her."

"Let her go, Elijah," Chase said, keeping the alarm out of his voice.

"I'm surprised you recognize me," Elijah said, backing up a step.

"It would be hard not to. Your face is still on wanted posters across the entire state."

"Then you know what I'm capable of doing. And listen carefully, because here's what's going to happen. I'm going to get off the train with her, and you're not going to do anything to stop me. Because if you do, well. . ." The man smiled. "She'll be another mess for you to clean up."

Chase kept his voice steady. "You won't get away with this. The train is full of undercover security. Drop the gun and end this now."

Elijah shook his head. "Sorry. This isn't a negotiation. I don't have time for games."

Chase felt the impact of the bullet as it burned across

his side. He stumbled backward in the aisle, his body slamming against something as he fought to catch his breath. Pain radiated through his torso, until the shouting voices around him faded into the darkness.

CHAPTER TWO

CHASE OPENED his eyes and tried to figure out where he was. It took a few more seconds before he realized he was lying on the floor of the train car, staring up at the ceiling. He had no idea how long he'd been there. Seconds. . .minutes. All he knew was that he'd been on the train with Jace, they'd been advised of a possible train heist, and then he'd recognized Elijah Duke.

The man involved in the shooting of his father-in-law, Garrett McQuaid.

"Hey. . . sir?"

Chase recognized the man crouching next to him as one of the passengers.

"My name's Simon. Are you okay?"

Chase hesitated, not sure how to answer the question. His ribcage throbbed, and from the splitting headache, he was pretty sure he'd hit his head as well.

"Where's Elijah?" he asked.

"The man with the gun?"

Chase nodded.

"He ran off."

"And his hostage?"

"She shaken up, but she'll be fine. My wife's with her right now."

"I need to go after him," Chase said, attempting to sit up.

"Hold on." Simon pressed his hands against Chase's shoulders. "I'm no doctor, but that man shot you."

Chase followed Simon's gaze to his side where blood seeped through his shirt.

He shook his head. "It's just a scratch. I'm fine."

"That isn't just a scratch."

Chase started to argue again, except he was afraid the man was right, and he wasn't fine. But that didn't matter right now.

"I need you to help me up. I've got to find my brother."

And stop Elijah.

He finally managed to stand up then pulled up the bottom of his shirt where a closer look convinced him the bullet had just grazed the skin.

"Have you seen the conductor?" Chase reholstered his gun that had fallen, then gripped the back of the seat as he tried to find his balance.

"No, but there was an announcement a minute ago. They want everyone to disembark as quickly as possible."

After grabbing his backpack, Chase stumbled down the aisle of the passenger car behind the man, still feeling off balance. Outside, the air smelled of oil and something acidic. He stepped off the train and blinked a few times, trying to clear his vision while he took in the scene around him. Dozens of passengers stood in the cold, most looking lost and confused. Further down the tracks he saw where the front engine had derailed and slid into a ditch.

With no sign of his brother, Chase strode toward Nate, who stood in the middle of the chaos, trying to calm the passengers.

"Chase. . .are you okay?" Nate asked, pulling him aside. "I heard a gunshot."

Chase pulled back his jacket, showing him the flesh wound, but that was the least of his worries at the moment. "I know who's behind this."

"It doesn't matter," Nate said, the panic obvious in his voice. "They had two fueled jeeps waiting, and are long gone by now." He glanced behind him. "They managed to derail the engine."

Chase frowned. It was a well-planned out heist, straight out of the play book of Jesse James and the Newton Boys.

A coyote howled in the distance as Chase searched the growing crowd of passengers. "Have you seen Jace?"

"No, but he's got to be here somewhere."

"What can I do?" Chase asked, still scanning the crowd for his brother.

"We're working on a head count—hold on," Nate said.

One of the uniformed security officers ran up to them. "They took a hostage by gunpoint into a jeep. It happened so fast, there was no way to stop them."

Chase stared down the track, wanting to ignore his gut.

"What was the hostage wearing?" he asked.

"I don't know. . ." The man hesitated. "A brown and orange plaid jacket—"

"That's my brother-in-law." Chase turned back to Nate,

a plan already formulating despite his throbbing head. "You've got a stock car with horses, don't you?"

"Yes, but—"

"I'm going to need help, but if we go after them now by horseback, we can track them."

"Hold on." Nate held up his hand. "I'm sorry, but I can't afford to send any of my men with you. Their job is the security of the train and its passengers, and right now we're sitting ducks to anyone else who might show up. On top of that, I have an injured engineer and passengers."

"They took my brother-in-law," Chase said, determined to plead his case.

"Trust me. I'd help if I could, but like I said, right now my priority at this moment has to be the train and its passengers."

"Then will you let me use one of the horses?" Chase asked.

"Get him what he needs," Nate said to the security guard. Then he turned back to Chase. "I know it's not enough, but I have to deal with this mess. You should be able to follow their tracks fairly easily. We should be less than ten miles from the Alpine station if that helps orient you."

Chase thanked the man then hurried down the tracks toward the stock car with the security guard. Tracking the men would be the easy part. Stopping them and bringing them in without anyone else getting hurt would be the challenging part. Because it was never enough. No matter how hard they worked, too often it felt as if the good guys always fell short. But if he didn't find Jace and get the medicine back to Hope. . .

Chase headed out five minutes later, his head still

pounding. He picked up the pace, thankful he could follow the tracks of the Jeep, but darkness was going to fall in a couple hours, bringing with it another layer of danger. Traveling through this area, especially alone, always posed some threats. Not only was there the possibility of hypothermia from the cold, or getting lost, there were also plenty of animals, like coyotes, mountain lions, and rattlesnakes. And then of course there was the constant lawlessness. Traveling alone was always discouraged, but if nothing else, he could head to Shadow Ridge and get a team together to come back and track down the men.

He scanned the terrain, looking for a familiar landmark, but he still wasn't sure exactly where he was. He kept following the jeeps' tracks, while ignoring his throbbing side, and let his mind settle on Hope. After ten days away, he missed her. He'd learned to rely on her not only for her company and conversation, but also for her wisdom.

All that had happened with the grid going down had changed things for everyone. For Hope and himself, it separated them for months until they'd finally found each other again. And while he didn't regret everything he'd done to stop the Realm, he'd almost lost her because of it.

His mind kept slipping away from the present as he followed the tracks, taking him back to that night when they'd stood together beneath the vast night sky and soaked in the ribbon of stars above them.

"We've both been through so much," he'd said, holding her hand. "The loss of your mother. Both of us trying to keep a community together, not to mention you were just kidnapped and shot."

"There are no guarantees, are there?" she'd said.

"No. Not beyond the simple fact that I love you."

"I feel like we've just been given another chance." She'd looked up at him with those wide eyes that never failed to stir his heart. "So what happens now?"

"I was thinking about a church wedding, and then settling down somewhere close to the clinic. Jace said he could use my help, especially during the transition as the power comes back on."

"As long as we're together, I don't care where we are or what's going on in the rest of the world. I'm content to simply be with you," she said.

The piercing howl of a coyote yanked him out of the past. The temperature was dropping, and he was finding it harder and harder to follow the tracks of the jeep. He clenched the reins as he ducked beneath a low branch. And that wasn't his only problem. He pressed his hand against his side and felt the sticky spot. It was bleeding again. A wave of dizziness swept through him, and he slowed down at the familiar fork in the road. If he was right, he wasn't far from Hangman's Ridge. Heading north would lead him toward the McQuaid ranch. South would continue following the jeeps' tracks.

He needed to make a decision.

He tried to clear the fog from his brain. He had no idea how far the men planned to drive. More than likely they had a location where they could store the goods, and it probably wasn't that far. Already the shadows were growing deeper around him, and they would want to be there by dark.

Come home, Chase.

He pressed his hand against his forehead at the sound of Hope's voice. He looked around, realizing that he wasn't thinking straight. Hope wasn't here. She was home, waiting for him. Not only was he hurt, he'd left the train with only what he had in his pack—water and some dried meat, but how long would that last him? And if a storm moved in, or the temperature continued to drop, he was going to be in trouble.

He gripped the reins tighter. He was letting fear take over. He'd faced situations far worse than this. He just had to think. The smarter decision would be to head to his family ranch on the outskirts of Shadow Ridge. Once there, he could put a posse together so he wasn't searching for Jace or facing the Duke brothers by himself.

But first he needed to make it home alive without getting stranded out here in the frigid weather.

CHAPTER THREE

Hope McQuaid Beckett rode across the edge of the McQuaid River Ranch on her appaloosa toward her father's house, the home she grew up in. Even at the beginning of winter, the surrounding views were stunning. Her family had settled on the two-hundred-acre ranch over a hundred years ago, and today, most of the land was still just as rugged and untouched as it had been a century ago. Views of open land with mountains in the background always brought with them a sense of nostalgia and almost made it possible to forget just how much things had changed in the past two years.

Almost.

The urgent message she'd received from Tess about Margaret's health was yet another reminder of just how volatile life had become. Margaret had become like family and a second mother to Hope after losing her mom. Margaret was also the woman she was certain her father was in love with. But now Margaret's symptoms were back, proof—unfortunately—that Hope's diagnosis was right.

At least Chase would be back this afternoon. The telegram she'd received from him this morning had assured her that not only was he coming home but also that he'd been successful in sourcing the medications she needed for Margaret and the others. She drew in a deep breath, trying to shake the growing anxiety. Despite her concerns over Margaret's health, there was something calming about being in the shadows of the distant mountains paired with the surrounding grasslands and groves of pine and oak trees. This was home, and even though things had changed tremendously, she couldn't imagine being anywhere else. She pulled slightly on the reins of her mare as the two-story ranch house came into sight with its long veranda and row of large windows facing the spectacular views.

She'd never planned to return to her childhood home, preferring the big city over the isolation of west Texas. And yet when circumstances had brought her here, she'd moved back thinking she could make a difference working in a place where medical care was harder to access. The grid going down had only managed to make a difficult situation impossible. They'd quickly run out of antibiotics, pain medicine, and other essential medications, and the lack of resources and access to information had changed everything. With the help of a few older residents in town, her own medical books, and the library, they'd planted medicinal gardens and implemented other emergency protocols, but she still felt out of control.

Or maybe she'd never really been in control at all.

Her thoughts shifted momentarily as Ranger, her father's German shepherd, ran toward her as she approached the house. Her younger sister, Tess, was out sweeping the front porch, dressed in jeans and a flowy blouse, with her long hair tied back. Like everyone, Tess's dreams had shifted in their trajectory when the grid when down, but in the process, Hope had watched her sister find a way to harness her passion and creativity.

Hope dismounted from her horse, tied the lead along the front porch rail, and then gave Ranger a proper hello before grabbing her medical bag and hurrying up the steps. "I got your message that Margaret isn't doing well today."

Tess held the broom in front of her and shook her head. "For the last few days most of her symptoms have been gone, but today she woke up in a lot of pain and with a fever."

Hope frowned. While she wasn't surprised, it wasn't the news she wanted to hear. "Unfortunately, from everything I've read, this illness seems to go in cycles," she said.

"Do you still think it's an issue with non-pasteurized dairy products?" Tess asked.

"That's my best guess after all the research I've done. I haven't found the source, but she's not the only one sick."

"That's what I've heard," Tess said.

News of possible tainted dairy products had spread fast through town and the surrounding area, adding with it another layer of fear. While confirming her findings might not be possible, she'd unofficially diagnosed Margaret and the others with brucellosis. She knew from her research that it was called a number of other things, like Malta fever or Mediterranean fever, but the bottom line was it came from unpasteurized milk from infected animals, or being in close contact with them.

An *unofficial* diagnosis that had her worried.

From everything she'd read from her own medical books and those at the library, the incubation period varied between days and months, but she'd had six patients over the past few weeks with similar symptoms that included chills, fever, and joint pain. She'd experimented without success trying to come up with an electricity-free system that would allow her to do conventional blood cultures. This left her having to rely on her instincts.

The cure for brucellosis had been simple at one time—a dose of antibiotics combined with a daily intramuscular injection. But if Chase didn't get back soon with the drugs, the outcome could be serious.

"Any news from Chase?" Tess asked as they walked into the house.

"A telegram this morning. He and Jace are supposed to arrive at the Alpine station this afternoon. Gideon is planning to pick them up with one of the wagons."

"That's great news."

"Yes, it is."

Hope shivered as she crossed the tile flooring. Without heating or cooling, the house seemed particularly cold this afternoon. She opted to keep her long coat on as she glanced around the spacious living room that opened up to the dining room. Both sides had large windows that gave enough light during the daytime, while the candles and lanterns scattered around the room were used when the sun began to set and night came.

Tess turned around to face her. "You seem worried."

"I'm worried about possible damage to Margaret's heart. She should have started the treatment weeks ago."

Untreated, the bacterial infection could affect the heart and even destroy the heart valves.

"And until Chase and my brother return, I'm going to worry." Hope forced a smile. "I realize that ordinary things take so much longer and that just because the trains are running doesn't mean the country is back on track."

Hope stopped in the entrance of the kitchen where the table had been covered with newspaper and a couple dozen small plates.

"Wow. . .what is all this?" Hope set her medical bag down then picked up one of the plates that was covered with a pile of fine orange powder.

"It's part of my paint pigment collection. All natural and sourced around here. All I have to do now is mix it with an additive so it can become paint."

"Really? Wow." Hope turned back to her sister. "Is this for one of your classes at the Book Nook?"

Tess shook her head. "Josie and I recently started going every week to help at Selena's school. This week, we're going to show them how to use natural pigments."

Selena Quinn had made an incredible impact in the community when she started a school in one of the run-down apartment complexes. Finding space for a school close to the apartments had been just as challenging as growing gardens and raising animals, but the rewards had been huge for the students.

"I'm proud of you, little sister."

Tess blushed. "I'm not sure why. Most of the time art seems so frivolous. I can't help but wonder if I should be spending more of my time. . .I don't know. . .helping you at the hospital or doing something more important at the school."

"It's hardly frivolous. Mr. O'Connor was right when he opened up the studio for you to teach and continue with your artwork. We all need a break from what's going on. A place to momentarily escape. People need a taste of normal more than ever in their lives."

Tess folded her arms across her chest. "I don't see you slowing down and taking a break."

"That's not a hundred percent true," Hope said, scrambling for an answer. "Morgan is. . . She's actually teaching me how to play the guitar."

"Wow. I'm impressed," Tess said. "You'll have to play at one of her open mike nights at the restaurant."

"Trust me." Hope chuckled as she picked her bag back up. "I'm not anywhere close to being ready to play in front of people."

"One day," Tess said with a grin as she headed toward the wood stove in the corner of the room. "I'll make some tea while you go check on Margaret."

Shadows clung to the walls as Hope headed up the familiar staircase then down the hallway that was filled with family photos, mainly of her and her siblings. Tess had been right about one thing. She hadn't been good at slowing down, but what choice did she have? By the time she was finished for the day at the clinic, all she wanted to do was spend a few moments with Chase, and sleep. And then, half the nights, it seemed, she was called out for an emergency.

Hope paused in front of the door of the guest bedroom where Margaret had been staying the past few weeks, making it easier for Tess to take care of her. This wasn't the first time Hope had been faced with a medical crisis that stretched her knowledge, but this felt. . .personal.

She knocked on the door, then paused when no one answered.

"Margaret?" she called, knocking again.

When there was still no answer, she opened the door a few inches. Margaret was sitting in a rocking chair next to the window, with her eyes closed.

Hope walked across the room and opened the curtains halfway, letting some of the afternoon light into the darkened space.

"Hope. . ." Margaret smiled groggily up at her, her long gray hair pulled up into a messy bun. "I must have fallen asleep."

"That's okay. You need the rest." Hope gave the older woman a hug then sat down on the bed across from her. "Tell me how you're doing."

"I thought I was doing better," Margaret said, leaning back in the chair. "The fever and most of my symptoms have been gone for days, but then last night. . . The pain and the fever started up again."

"What about your headaches?"

"I haven't had one for three or four days. Not until this morning."

"I was hoping your lack of symptoms was going to turn out to be a good sign, but from my research, periods of remission are normal."

"And the complications?"

Hope hesitated as she pulled the blood pressure cuff out of her bag and secured it on Margaret's arm. "Most people don't have any serious complications."

At least that was what she was praying.

The drugs Chase was bringing her should prevent relapse as well as issues with the heart. As long as it wasn't too late.

Hope studied Margaret's solemn expression, worried she was missing something as she continued to take her vitals. Besides the physical symptoms, there were often connected emotional responses, like depression, insomnia, and irritability. So far, she hadn't noted any emotional instabilities, but she couldn't let anything slip by.

"Is there something else?" Hope asked, as she listened to Margaret's heart.

The older woman glanced toward the window, her lips pressed together.

"Margaret?"

She finally looked back at Hope. "You've got enough on your plate. I don't want you worrying any more than you already are."

"You don't worry about me," Hope said, squeezing the woman's hand. "Tell me what's going on."

Margaret fiddled with the tassels of the crocheted blanket on her lap before speaking again. "I wouldn't say anything, but. . . It's actually your father I'm worried about."

"Dad?" Hope sat back, surprised at the woman's confession. "What do you mean?"

"I don't know. He's been. . .different lately. He's pulled away from me, and I can't figure out why."

Hope's mind shifted to last Sunday. Even with Chase and her brother gone, the McQuaid family had dinner together after church like they normally did. She hadn't noticed anything out of the ordinary then, or this last week when she'd had lunch with him at the restaurant. But she also knew that she'd been busy at the clinic, working extra hours with Chase gone, and how easy it was to get caught up in her own world.

What had she missed?

"What else?" Hope asked.

"I know how hard it was the first year. He pretty much gave up. I've always said that there isn't a timetable for grief, but he lost so much that year that it left him without a purpose."

"You don't think he's better now?"

"I've thought he was, until recently."

"Okay," Hope said. "Explain."

"Maybe I'm wrong," Margaret said, clearly not liking the direction of the conversation.

"It's okay. Go ahead."

Margaret let out a deep breath. "I realize that losing Katherine was devastating for him, and I would never think I could take her place. She was my best friend. Maybe I read things wrong. Felt things I shouldn't have, while believing he feels the same for me. I think I was wrong. I actually thought he was going to ask me to marry him."

"But he hasn't."

"No." Margaret looked up, shaking her head. "I'm sorry. I shouldn't have brought this up, it's just that I honestly feel like such a fool. And now I'm getting myself worked up for nothing, but we haven't really talked for weeks. He's always busy and in a hurry with some sort of excuse."

"The two of you have been through a lot together," Hope said, not sure what her response should be.

"I never expected to fall in love again, least of all with your father. All I can figure out is that I'm wrong and that he never felt the same way."

"I've seen the way he looks at you. I know he cares about you," Hope said.

"As more than just a close friend?"

"I don't know, but it seems to me like you need to talk to him."

Margaret looked away toward the window. "I know. I. . .I guess I'm just afraid to find out the truth. You're father isn't exactly a man of many words."

Hope let out a soft laugh. "No, and I also know that sometimes my father needs a little push now and then."

While she'd never spoken to her father about his feelings toward Margaret, something told her that Margaret hadn't imagined them. Hope watched him light up when he was around her. But she also knew that he'd changed. All of them had.

"Even if I'm right about how he feels about me," Margaret continued, turning back to Hope, "I'm not sure he's dealt with all of his grief. And I'm not sure that we can move forward until he does."

Hope took Margaret's hand and squeezed it, knowing there was a chance the woman was right. It had taken her brother Jace a long time to convince their father to go back to work, and months of physical therapy. But it had been the emotional toll that had ripped away her dad's motivation. He'd been doing so much better, but if something had happened to dig up those feelings again. . .

Hope tried to put her thoughts in order. "Maybe he's afraid of losing you like. . .like he lost Mom."

"I've thought of that. But if that's true, I don't want to be the one who triggers him." Margaret waved off the conversation. "I shouldn't have bothered you with this, because you're right. I need to talk to him. And I will."

"Good. I really think you should," Hope said, standing up. "And in the meantime, why don't I get you some tea.

Tess is heating up the water, and I know I could use some as well. It's chilly in here."

Margaret nodded. "I'd like that. Thank you."

Hope fought back the tears as she stepped out of Margaret's room and headed back toward the kitchen. She'd seen the pain in the older woman's eyes as they'd talked about her father and Margaret's relationship, but that wasn't the only thing that had her concerned. Something was different this time when she'd listened to Margaret's heart. There was a new whooshing sound, which meant there was a chance that the bacterial disease had inflamed her heart. And if the valves had been damaged or destroyed, there was nothing else she could do to help Margaret.

CHAPTER FOUR

Jace squinted at the light as someone ripped the hood off his head. He waited for his eyes to adjust to the brightness, then tried to get his bearings now that he was out of the jeep. There were three men. One stood next to him, still gripping his arm. He recognized the other two standing in front of him from wanted posters.

The Duke brothers.

He let out a sharp huff of air. As far as he knew, the brothers had no idea he was Garrett McQuaid's son, but that didn't make him feel any better about the situation.

"What were you thinking, taking a hostage, you fool?" Elijah Duke's bearded face turned red with anger.

The tall, skinny man who'd grabbed Jace dug his fingers deeper into his arm at Elijah's outburst. "What are they going to do about it? This is still the Wild West. Garrett McQuaid's been looking for you for two years and never picked up your trail. It's not like they're going to be able to track us down. Besides, I figured a hostage could come in handy."

"The plan was a train heist. Grab the goods and get out. That was it."

Jace took in his surroundings while the men continued to argue. There were the two jeeps to his left and a lone cabin ahead to his right. The men had already started hauling the supplies they'd taken from the train and unloading them onto the porch. He didn't recognize the area that was thick with trees, but he could narrow down the location. From the train, they'd driven a good twenty, maybe thirty minutes, which put them somewhere between Alpine and Shadow Ridge. He needed a plan, but knowing the reputation of these men guaranteed escape wasn't going to be easy. They'd shot his father in cold blood, and he knew they wouldn't hesitate to do the same with him.

"What do you want me to do with him?"

Jace turned back to the men at the question, not sure he wanted to hear their response.

"I want you to dispose of him, Wyatt, because—"

"I might be able to help you," Jace said, scrambling for a way to change the man's mind.

"I highly doubt that," Elijah said.

"You might as well let him talk." Adam, the younger Duke brother, spoke up for the first time.

"I can understand that you're disappointed with your take," Jace said. "But the money was never on that train. There was just passengers, some medical supplies, and luggage."

Adam glanced at his brother, then back at Jace. "You're telling me we had the wrong train?"

"Your information was wrong, wasn't it?" Jace said.

Elijah rubbed the back of his neck, clearly irritated. "It

doesn't matter. The medicine can be sold on the black market for a decent take. We can always hit another train."

"And take another chance of missing the payroll cash that they've started moving by rail?"

Elijah took a step forward. "How would you know which trains are carrying the payrolls?"

"I was working security on the train."

"Prove it," Elijah said.

Jace held the man's gaze. "In the secured luggage compartment you tried to rob, there were four crates of medicine, two dozen or so suitcases, but no cash or other valuables in the car."

"My informant said there was going to be a bank payroll on that train," Elijah countered.

"And now you know your informant was wrong," Jace said. "You can't trust just anyone."

Elijah spit on the ground, inches from Jace's feet. "Don't be cocky with me. You're going to be lucky if you actually get out of this alive. I don't *have* to mess with you. I could end it right now."

"True, but there are lot of people shipping valuables now that the grid is coming back up again. You just have to make sure you have the right information, and that information, I believe, should be worth my life."

"What have we got to lose?" Wyatt asked.

"Time, and my patience." Elijah said. "Tie him up for now, but if I find out you're lying, you'll end up with a bullet in your head."

CHAPTER FIVE

Hope had just set the tray of empty teacups on the kitchen counter when she heard the front door open, followed by a loud squeal. She turned toward the living room as the blond-haired eight-year-old dashed past, nearly running into her.

"Noah," Hope said, jumping out of the way.

"I'm looking for Ranger," he said, spinning around to face her, his hands on his hips and his expression serious. "Do you know where he is?"

"Noah. . ." his mother, Morgan McQuaid, prompted from the doorway.

Noah held up the plastic backpack he was carrying and looked up at Hope. "I'm sorry, but I have a bone for Ranger."

"That explains the urgency." Hope laughed as she leaned against the counter. "He's going to be one happy canine."

A year ago, her brother Jace married widowed and single mom Morgan, and as the first grandchild, Noah added energy and life to their family.

"Do you know where he is?" Noah asked again.

"I haven't seen him since I got here. He's probably taking a nap."

"I'll help you find him," Tess said, walking into the room with a candle to light a couple of the lanterns.

Morgan turned to Noah. "Listen to your aunt Tess and stay close to the house. It's going to be dark soon."

Morgan waited until Noah had gone outside before turning back to Hope. "Since you're here by yourself, I'm assuming our husbands haven't made it back yet."

Hope shook her head, trying not to worry at the reminder. "Gideon went to the train station to pick them up, but no. Not yet."

Morgan frowned. "They should be here by now."

"I know." Hope glanced out the window at the sinking sun. "I'm worried something happened to delay them."

"How is Margaret?" Morgan set the box she'd been holding onto the counter before turning back to Hope.

Hope shook her head. "She's got a fever, and her joint pain is getting worse."

Morgan folded her arms in front of her. "Then break it down for me. What do you need, and what are your alternatives?"

Hope let out a sigh, grateful for her sister-in-law, who was always willing to think outside the box. "Besides the medications I need, I don't think there is an alternative. I haven't said anything to Margaret, or even to Tess for that matter, but one of the complications is endocarditis."

"Which is?" Morgan asked.

"The inflammation of the inner lining of the heart."

Hope paused. "I found an irregularity in Margaret's heartbeat today."

"Which is a sign of. . .endocarditis?"

Hope nodded.

"Maybe your diagnosis is wrong. That would be understandable without access to labs."

"It's always possible, but she has all the classic symptoms. Sweating, joint and muscle pain, and now the heart issue. With signs of the infection progressing, I'm running out of options for her." Hope didn't even try to stop the bubbling panic. "Unless our husbands can get me what I need—"

"Hope, stop." Her sister-in-law crossed the tile floor and took her hands. "This isn't your fault. Ultimately, you don't have control over this."

She frowned, knowing that Morgan was right, but she wasn't ready to step back from the situation. "It doesn't matter whose fault it is. I have patients who need me. Margaret needs me, and yet I can't do anything to fix this."

"You're too hard on yourself. I've watched you these past two years. You've made a difference in the lives of so many."

Then why does it never seem to be enough?

"I'm worried about how much longer Margaret can wait for the medicine, but I'm also worried about our husbands. They should be here," Hope said.

"I know." Morgan glanced at the box she'd brought in with her. "When is the last time you ate something?"

Hope glanced at the empty teacups. "I just had a tea break with Margaret and Tess."

"Did you eat breakfast or lunch?"

Hope's stomach turned at the thought of food. "I honestly haven't been hungry."

"I'll take that as a no," Morgan said. "Lucky for you, a bone for Ranger isn't the only thing we brought. I brought some hot chicken soup from the diner, as well as homemade blueberry muffins. There's plenty of both."

Hope breathed in the scent of onions, garlic, and broth as Morgan pulled out a large Tupperware bowl from a cooler box. "How is the café doing? I'm sorry I haven't dropped by for a while."

"It's doing great, actually. Ava's been amazing. She has a knack of being creative in the kitchen which we need right now."

Before the grid went down, Morgan ran a restaurant with some of the best pies and barbecue around. Late last year, along with their sister-in-law Ava, Levi's wife, Morgan decided to reopen the café. It gave the town a place to eat as well as allow local musicians to play on the front stage, becoming yet another piece of healing and bringing the town together.

Morgan held up one of the muffins.

"That does look delicious," Hope said, smiling for the first time.

"Oh, it is."

Her stomach growled, and she realized just how hungry she was until the sudden wave of nausea hit.

Another layer of stress added to the mix. She wasn't just worried about her own health.

She brushed her hand against her stomach then pushed away the fear. It was all going to be okay. Chase and her brother were going to get the medicine they needed. She would simply be extra careful to insure she didn't get infected.

"I think I'm pregnant," she blurted out.

"Wait. What?" Morgan squealed. "How far along?"

"Not far."

"How do you know?"

Hope pulled out a chair from the kitchen table as a wave of fatigue swept over her.

With no actual pregnancy tests, there was no way to know yet. Not a hundred percent anyway.

"I took a test. Well, an Egyptian DIY test." Hope shrugged. "I might've gotten a bit distracted at the library, but there's so much interesting information, it's easy to go down a rabbit hole."

"Wait." Morgan grabbed a muffin, took a bite, and sat down next to her. "You said Egyptian?"

Hope tugged on the end of her ponytail. Why did hearing it out loud make it sound so ridiculous? "Apparently, even back in the 1300s, urine-based pregnancy tests were a thing."

"What did you have to do?" Morgan asked, clearly intrigued by the direction of the conversation.

Hope cleared her throat. "They say if you pee on wheat or barley seeds you can find out if you're pregnant. If the barley sprouts, it's going to be a boy, and if the wheat sprouts, it's going to be a girl."

"And if you're not pregnant?"

"Then the seeds don't sprout."

Morgan took another bite. "How accurate is this?"

"Someone tested the theories back in the sixties and found that it was about 70 percent accurate."

Morgan let out a squeal. "I'm so excited. Does Chase know?"

Hope shook her head. "I just found out. With the women who have come to me over the past two years, I've had them wait until I could confirm with a physical exam, but—"

"You're not that patient."

"Thanks, but true." Hope sat back in her chair and laughed, but her smile didn't last. "But. . .as happy as I am, I'm worried."

"Because of the bacterial infection."

Hope nodded. "I'm being careful, but it is possible for the infection to spread through the air."

"And you're afraid you could catch it." Morgan leaned forward. "You need to stop treating those patients, Hope. Surely someone else can do it."

She'd already tried to come up with another solution, but it wasn't that simple. "There are certain symptoms I'm looking for that someone else might not catch. I'll be careful."

"Then we just have to keep praying that the men will be back soon, Margaret will get her medicine, and your baby will be fine."

"And if they're not able to get everything I need?" Hope's gaze dropped as she tried to stop the waves of panic. "One of my patients is pregnant and the infection can cause miscarriages."

This time the silence between them lingered.

"I know this is hard," Morgan finally said, "but worrying isn't going to help. I trust my husband, and yours as well. They'll get what you need."

Hope glanced down at her uneaten muffin, knowing

Morgan was right. She shouldn't worry, and yet so much rested on her shoulders. She wasn't sure how *not* to worry. The infection was already spreading, and so far she'd hadn't been able to determine the source of the outbreak.

And if she didn't find a way to stop this.

If something happened to their baby...

She drew in a sharp breath. "I'm trying to have faith and not get caught up in the roller coaster of doubt, but I'm scared, Morgan. Not only am I in the middle of dealing with an infectious disease, but this world...how am I supposed to handle raising a child and running the clinic?"

It was a question she hadn't really let herself fully consider up to this point, and the answers terrified her.

"The same way we've been handling things for the last two years. We all come together and help each other. We cover for each other. None of that will change. And when the lights come back on, we keep working to get life back to normal."

"I don't know." She picked at the muffin. "Maybe it's hormones, but it all seems completely overwhelming."

"None of this took God by surprise," Morgan said, squeezing Hope's hand. "Not even the grid going down. Your baby will be loved and cared for."

"I know." On one level at least. Hope brushed away an unwanted tear. "I want this child—more than anything—but I'm afraid to bring him or her into a world that's so unstable. And I have a feeling that it's going to get worse before it gets better."

They'd both heard the rumors. Rumors of unrest across the country, even as the grid started to come back on. Rebuilding the state and country was going to take time.

"I'm just tired of feeling as if my hands are tied," Hope said as she looked up and caught Morgan's gaze.

"Mom?" Noah rushed into the house—slower than the last time—with Tess trailing behind. "Mr. Gideon's here."

"He is?" Hope jumped up from her chair and hurried to the door.

She stepped out onto the veranda as Gideon was walking up the steps, and felt her heart stop.

"You're alone?" She held her hand up to block the sun that had just dropped against the horizon. "Where are the men?"

"And the medicine?" Morgan added, stepping up behind her.

Gideon took the last step then glanced down at the ground, avoiding their gaze. "I honestly don't know."

Morgan shook her head. "What do you mean, you don't know? The telegram said they'd be in this afternoon on the westbound train."

Gideon shoved his hands into his pockets. "When I got to the station, I was told that the train was delayed and to come back in the morning for an update."

"Did they say why?" Hope asked.

"No," Gideon said.

Hope felt the rising panic. "You're not telling us something."

Gideon cleared his throat. "I stopped by town before coming out here, just in case they were there or maybe someone knew something about the delay."

"And?" Hope prompted.

"A runner just arrived in town," Gideon said, finally looking up at them. "According to witnesses, the train was attacked a few miles east of Alpine."

CHAPTER SIX

CHASE TRIED to ignore the searing pain in his side, but the uneven motion of the horse's gait made him feel as if it were on fire. He clenched his jaw against the pain. All he had to do was make it another half mile to the ranch, but he was worried about how much damage had been done. And even more worried about what had happened to Jace.

Guilt pressed against his chest over the fact that he'd decided not to continue searching for Jace, but he knew he'd made the right choice. There was no way he would have been able to take down the Duke brothers on his own in this condition.

He focused on the outline of the ranch house once it finally appeared in the distance in the moonlight. In the darkness, he couldn't see much of the orchards and ranch land around him, but at least he'd made it back in one piece. He just needed Hope to be here.

While he and Hope lived in a house in town near the clinic, the ranch had become an oasis for both of them whenever they were able to grab a few hours away from work. After living in Boston, he realized how much he appreciated the slower west Texas pace. There was something about the open grasslands, juniper savannas, and distant mountain slopes that were covered with piñon pine and oak. Unlike the McQuaid family, he hadn't always lived here, but that didn't mean he didn't see it as home.

He extended his legs, trying to shift his position on the saddle. He wasn't sure he could make it all the way to the clinic in town, and from the throbbing pain, he knew he needed medical care. Hope should be at the ranch. She normally spent most of her days at the clinic in town, but with Margaret's declining health, she'd started going to the ranch in the evenings so she could check on her.

He worried about her. As the only doctor for seventy-plus miles, her role had been difficult before the grid went down. Now, with no electricity and few resources, things were even more difficult. She'd spread herself too thin, and even with news that the power should be coming back on soon, he didn't see her workload easing.

Thoughts of Hope always made him smile. She'd been the first girl he'd fallen in love with and the first girl who'd broken his heart. Finding her again after a decade-plus apart was the best thing that ever happened to him. She'd stolen his heart at eighteen, and she was still the one who knew how to make him laugh.

Chase pulled back on the reins then let out a sharp breath of relief as he finally rode up to the covered veranda of the ranch house. Noah must have been looking out the window, because a second later, he ran out of the house with Ranger trailing behind him.

"Uncle Chase!" he called, running down the stairs. "You're back!"

Chase slowly dismounted then glanced down at the blood that had spread across his shirt. If Noah was here, more than likely his mother and Hope were here as well.

He needed Hope.

"Is your Aunt Hope here?" he asked. He secured the horse then pulled on his jacket to cover the red patch of blood.

"She's inside with my mom. They've been waiting for you and my dad—"

The front door swung open again, and Hope ran down the steps toward him.

"Chase?"

Ranger started barking and running in circles as Chase pulled her into his arms, overwhelmed at the rush of emotions at seeing her again. "I've missed you so much."

"I've been worried," she said, looking up at him. She lowered her voice. "We heard the train was attacked."

He winced as she pressed in against his chest, wishing he didn't have to tell her that he'd not only failed to bring back the medicine, but he didn't know where Jace was.

"Chase. . .what's wrong?" She took a step backward in the moonlight and looked down at his side. "You're hurt."

"I know."

Hope frowned, clearly not impressed with his trying to minimize the situation. "What happened?"

He hesitated. "It's a gunshot wound, but it's really not serious."

She shook her head. "There's no such thing as a gunshot wound that isn't serious."

"It's just a graze, though my favorite coat now has a bullet hole through it. You can look at it, but I'm fine."

She touched his shirt. "You're not fine, and where's Jace?"

Chase caught the panic in her voice. He glanced at Noah, who was still distracted by Ranger. There was no way he could discuss what had happened in front of the boy.

"I need to talk to you and Morgan."

"Samuel's running security on the ranch tonight," Hope said, stepping back and taking charge as if she were back in the ER. "I'll send him into town to get Dad and Kellan. They need to hear what's going on as well. Tess can hang out with Noah."

She pulled out a solar-powered walkie-talkie from her pocket and called the night guard they'd hired a few months ago when there had been an uptick of burglaries on local farms and ranches.

The line crackled as Samuel answered on the other end.

"Samuel," she said, "I need you to come to the house to take care of Chase's horse, and then go into town and bring Kellan and Dad back here."

"Yes, ma'am."

"And Samuel," she said. "Hurry."

Morgan stepped out of the house a moment later as Chase started up the porch steps with Hope.

"Chase. . .you're back." Morgan looked behind him as if expecting her husband to appear then dropped her hands to her sides when he didn't.

"Where's Tess?" Hope asked, rushing into the house ahead of them.

Morgan followed behind, looking confused.

"Tess," Hope said, addressing her sister who had just

walked into the room. "Margaret borrowed a few more books from the library and promised to read to Noah tonight. Do you mind?"

Tess glanced from Hope to Chase, then back to Hope again and nodded. "Of course not. How about it, champ? I saw the books she has, and you're going to love them."

Once the two of them had headed upstairs, Morgan didn't hesitate.

"Where's Jace?"

"I'm sorry, Morgan," he said. "I don't know."

"What do you mean, you don't know?" Morgan asked, her voice rising. "What happened out there?"

Chase winced as he sat down at the kitchen table while Hope grabbed her medical bag and moved two lanterns onto the table. He sat still for a moment, trying not to move as Hope pulled up the bottom of his shirt that was stuck to his skin from the dried blood.

"Give me a second," he said, taking her hand. "Morgan needs to know what's going on. Both of you do."

Hope nodded, then stepped back.

"We were on the train with the medicine and other goods secured in the luggage car when we found out from the conductor that there were rumors the train was going to be robbed," he said, still holding Hope's hand. "Jace and I were asked to help with security, but at least one of the outlaws was already on the train."

Morgan pulled up a chair and sat down in front of him. "That doesn't explain where Jace is."

"Or how you got shot," Hope added.

Chase nodded. "There was a standoff in one of the passenger cars—in the car I was in. A woman was taken hostage. That's when I got hit. The entire heist was well planned and happened fast. They somehow managed to stop the train and even derailed the front engine."

"And Jace?"

"I found out from one of the train's security guards that they took him at gunpoint. I tracked him as long as I could but eventually decided to come back here to get help."

"What?" Morgan's voice rose. "No, I can't—"

"Jace is resourceful," Chase said, trying to reassure Morgan. "More than likely, he'll show up here wondering where I am."

"And if he doesn't?" Morgan frowned then jutted out her chin, as if wanting to believe him, but not sure if she did. "How are we going to find him? They could have taken him anywhere."

Guilt resurfaced over his decision. "I know the direction they went, and I believe we can pick up the trail."

"I know you did what you thought was best." Morgan pressed her shoulders back and drew in a long breath. "But what if we can't find him? Do you have a description of the men? Any idea who they are or where they might have gone?"

"I know who shot me."

"What?" Hope sat down on the other side of Chase. "Who?"

He hesitated before answering, not sure what kind of reaction he was going to get. "It was Elijah Duke."

"Elijah Duke?" Hope leaned forward. "My father has been searching for him for two years. Ever since he got shot."

"I know," Chase said.

"How are you going to find him now?" Morgan asked.

"They left the train in two jeeps," Chase said. "There are no guarantees, I know, but I was able to track them almost to Hangman's Ridge. They probably stopped for the night. If we leave first thing in the morning, we should be able to pick up their tracks again."

Morgan didn't look convinced. "Those are a lot of assumptions. Plus, not only do they have vehicles and we only have horses, these men don't hesitate to eliminate anyone who gets in their way."

Chase nodded, knowing she was right. It wasn't the first time they'd organized a search party, but searching for bad guys was very different from searching for a missing person. And he knew enough about the Duke brothers to know that they wouldn't go down without a fight. They were going to have to be ready for anything.

"That's all true," Hope said, responding to Morgan. "But Chase is right. My father is one of the best trackers I know. He'll be able to track them, Morgan. Right now, though, I need to see what kind of damage the bullet did."

Morgan's hands shook as she stood up. "Finish patching up your husband. I'm going to check on Noah. We can make a plan as soon as Kellan and your dad get here."

Chase tried to sit still while Hope finished pulling back the shirt that was stuck to his side. She concentrated on what she was doing—brow furrowed, lips pressed together—completely focused. All familiar things about the woman he'd married.

"I missed you," he said.

"I missed you too, but hold still." She pushed back his hair from his forehead and frowned. "What happened here?"

"Hit my head on one of the seats when the train screeched to a halt. May or may not have gotten a concussion."

"Headache?"

"Yes," he said.

"Nausea or vomiting?"

"No."

'What about groggy or confused?"

"Not really. Mainly, I'm just tired."

She let out a huff of air.

"So what's the verdict, Doc?" he asked.

Hope set her hands on her hips. "For one, your wife is extremely glad you're alive and that you came back when you did. Two, the gunshot wound isn't near as bad as it could have been, but it still needs to be cleaned and bandaged. You'll have to be careful, because we can't allow it to get infected."

His heart revved up. "Can it wait?"

"Cleaning you up?"

He nodded.

"Why?" she asked, catching his gaze.

"Because I very much want to kiss you."

She leaned over and brushed her lips slowly against his. "I need to patch you up, or I won't be letting you go on that search party I know you'll insist on joining."

"After a good night's sleep, I'll be fine," Chase said, wishing he could go home with his wife and forget about all of this.

"You're stubborn, but I wouldn't want it any other way," she said, giving him one more lingering kiss with a wide grin. "Now let me do my job."

Hope had just finished cleaning him up and serving

him a bowl of soup when Kellan and his father-in-law arrived.

"Chase...I'm glad you made it back safe." Garrett pulled him into a hug then looked around the room. "Where's Jace?"

"Our train was hijacked," Chase said, getting straight to the point. "Jace was taken hostage."

"What?" Kellan asked. "By who?"

Chase glanced at his father-in-law, this time hesitating before answering. "Elijah Duke."

CHAPTER SEVEN

Elijah Duke.

The name felt like a punch in the gut to Garrett McQuaid.

He closed his eyes for a moment as the dark memories pressed in on him. He hadn't seen the man for almost two years, but he'd thought about him every single day. The moment he'd looked into the barrel of Elijah Duke's gun, Garrett had known the other man was going to pull the trigger. Known he was going to die. He remembered grabbing Elijah's Glock and flipping the man onto his back. Then he'd dug his boot into the man's backside so he could search the rocky terrain for his brother. The response had been a rifle shot from the ridge that took Garrett down.

Miraculously, Hope managed to patch him back together, but while he'd survived, he'd lost Kat in a separate incident when the grid went down that day. The trauma of that weekend had not only left him with long-term physical damage, but also with gaping holes in his memory.

He'd been told that Tess, Levi, and Jace had driven to Shadow Ridge to celebrate his and Kat's anniversary on Thursday afternoon. Kat ordered an extra slice of her favorite lemon meringue pie for the family dinner they'd had together that night. He didn't remember any of it.

His decision to go out alone to search for the Duke brothers Friday morning didn't come as a surprise to anyone. Law enforcement across the entire state had searched for the fugitives for six days while the men racked up a growing list of charges, tracking them all the way to the dusty West Texas landscape. Like most of the small towns dotting the map out here, law enforcement resources were stretched thin, and there hadn't been time to call for backup.

Then the grid had gone down, life had fallen apart, and he hadn't been able to fix any of it.

He drew in a deep breath, knowing that he didn't have time to mourn the past. Not if they were going to find Jace. And that wasn't the only thing they needed to do. Hope had made it clear that without the medicine for Margaret, there was no way to treat her infection.

Margaret.

His thoughts pulled him under again. He'd never meant to let his feelings for Margaret grow. Kat had always been the only one for him, but over the past weeks and months things began to change between him and his late wife's best friend until he'd realized that there might be room in his heart for someone else. That realization, though, terrified him, and the more his feelings grew, the more he'd found himself pulling back.

"Dad?"

"I'm sorry." He looked up at the sound of Hope's voice,

trying to rein his thoughts back to the present. "Are you sure it was the Duke brothers?"

"I know Elijah's involved," Chase said. "I'm assuming his brother is as well."

"They always worked together, usually bringing one or two others onto their team."

Garrett sat down at the kitchen table, suddenly feeling exhausted. He'd already had a long day dealing with a string of burglaries in town with one ending in an assault of the homeowner. Even with reports of the grid coming back on across the state, sometimes it felt as if they'd fallen into a dark hole with no way out. And even once power was reestablished, with limited resources, keeping crime in check would no doubt continue to be a challenge out here.

"Can I get you some of Morgan's soup, Dad? Kellan?" Hope asked, pausing the conversation. "There's plenty."

"I'll never pass up Morgan's cooking," Kellan said, joining Chase and Garrett at the table. "Thank you."

"Tell me exactly what happened," Garrett said, after taking a spoonful of the soup.

"There were three men," Chase said. "At least one who was on the train—Elijah—plus the ones who waited at the rendezvous point with two jeeps."

Garrett ate while Chase continued with an abbreviated account of what happened.

"I tracked them close to Hangman's Ridge where there's a fork in the trail, but at that point my side and head were throbbing, and I was worried I wouldn't make it. I decided to come straight to the ranch for help."

"You made the right decision," Garrett said, still trying

to shake past memories. "Those men have caused a reign of destruction across the entire state."

"And now they have my husband."

Garrett looked up as his daughter-in-law walked into the room. There were few people he knew who were as strong as Morgan. She'd lost her husband the same day he'd lost Kat. She'd worked hard to keep their greenhouses and beehives going, and her efforts had paid off. For two years now, she'd managed to produce crops that helped keep food not just on her table, but a large part of the community's. And on top of that, along with his other daughter-in-law, Ava, Morgan had reopened her restaurant, helping people feel like life was a little bit back to normal.

"We're going to find Jace," Garrett said as she sat down across from him.

"And if we don't?" Morgan said. "We know what these men are capable of."

Garrett didn't miss the fear in his daughter-in-law's eyes, and he understood her panic because he was feeling the same thing.

"I know this is hard, but we need to make a plan," Chase said, pushing his empty bowl away and turning to Garrett.

"Should we bring more people in for the search?" Hope asked.

"Normally, I would say yes," Garrett said, "but we're already spread thin in town, especially with this string of burglaries."

"I have to say I agree," Kellan said. "Plus, Levi's in Van Horn and won't be back for a couple days."

"Then we'll leave it to the three of us," Chase said. "If

we get there and it doesn't seem wise to try and take them down, we'll reconsider our next move."

"We need to be well rested," Garrett said. "Chase, why don't you and Hope spend the night here, so we can leave at first light."

Chase looked up at Hope. "Is that okay with you?"

"Of course."

"I'll see you all in the morning then," Garrett said, grabbing his bag that was sitting on the floor. "Tomorrow's going to be a long day."

He started toward his room. Maybe it was just the fatigue, but he was irritated at himself at how deeply the news of the Duke brothers had affected him.

Hope caught up to him halfway down the hallway. "Dad. . .are you okay?"

"Honestly," he said, turning around, "no. Hearing the Duke brothers are here has brought to the surface the nightmares of everything I lost." He caught her gaze in the glimmer of light from the lantern she was carrying. "But I'll be okay. Especially once they're taken into custody. I've been waiting for that day for a long time."

"I know. We all have," she said, resting her hand on his arm for a moment. "Listen. . . I know you're tired, but I think Margaret needs to see you before you go to bed. She had a rough day."

Garrett hesitated. He knew Hope was right and he should go talk to her. He'd been staying in town lately, which meant he missed dinner at the ranch most nights, and time with Margaret. He hadn't wanted her to know the guilt and second thoughts he'd been battling with the past few weeks.

"I'm tired, Hope. Tell her I'll see her when I get back,"

he said. "I need some sleep, and morning is going to come early."

"She needs you," Hope said.

Garrett let out a soft sigh. He loved his daughter, but there were times when he wished she would back off from trying to mother him. Even when she was right.

"Okay," he said. "I'll go tell her good night."

Five minutes later, he stopped at the closed door of Margaret's room and felt the familiar rush of anxiety spread through him. He'd come a long way, but that bullet had changed his life, leaving him scars that went deeper than a hole in his chest.

He knocked, then waited for her to answer. Inside Margaret's room, he tried not to notice how much she'd changed over the past few weeks. The infection zapped her of energy and left her in constant pain. She was sitting in the rocking chair next to a lantern, reading one of her favorite crime novels.

"Let me get you another blanket," he said, shoving away the doubts as far as he could. "It's cold in here."

She smiled up at him. "Thank you."

Her face was pale as he laid the quilt across her legs. Margaret had been the one who pulled him out of his depression. Who'd stuck with him through physical therapy, cooked and cleaned and kept the house going when he'd been lost. She'd helped to keep his family together in the middle of the world with no electricity, no cell phones, grocery stores, or Amazon delivery.

She'd helped him find himself again.

He'd never wanted to find love again, but wasn't that exactly what he'd found?

"Morgan told me about Jace," Margaret said. "I'm so sorry. I know this is hard on you."

"It is, but I'm also worried about the stolen medicine as well. I know you need it."

Margaret smiled up at him. "I'm just trusting God that he'll bring both Jace and the medicine safely to Shadow Ridge."

"Maybe," Garrett said, "but God doesn't always show up when we want him to."

He caught the disappointment in her eyes at his words, but he knew firsthand that God didn't always say yes, no matter how hard he prayed.

"God has managed to bring us through so much these past two years, Garrett." She pressed her hand against her heart. "And as much as you fight Him, He's still right here."

Garrett frowned. He knew she was right, but he'd lost so much. How was he supposed to just move on?

"How are you feeling today?" he asked, changing the subject.

"It's one of those days. Yesterday was a lot better. I'm frustrated because I have a lot I want to do."

"The only thing you have to worry about is getting better."

"Tess and the girls have been so helpful. I'm grateful."

His youngest daughter Tess, and her husband Kellan, had moved into the ranch house in order to help care for Margaret. He'd always been proud of his family, but the grid going down had managed to bring them all closer.

Another miracle.

He pushed the thought away.

"You're going after them," she said.

It was a question rather than a statement.

Any smile that it been in her expression vanished. And he was reminded once again of her frailty and how devastated he'd be to lose her.

"We're going to find Jace and the medicine and make sure you're okay," he said.

"Maybe when you get back, we could go for a walk. It's been a while since we really talked."

"I know, and I'm sorry," he said, looking for an excuse. "Things have been busy in town."

"I know." She smiled up at him. "Go on to bed. You have a long day ahead of you."

A moment later, he shut the door behind him and headed back downstairs. He should have stayed and talked. Assured her that he still cared.

Instead, he'd couldn't shake the feeling that he'd betrayed her.

CHAPTER EIGHT

Hope's shoulders ached as she finished cleaning up the dishes in the kitchen. Medically speaking, she knew high-stress situations created high levels of cortisol, and that the constant anxiety could take a toll on the body. She was also aware of the importance of dealing with said stress. But it wasn't always easy.

She picked up the plastic tub she'd used to wash the dishes then stepped outside to dumped the water. Morgan and Tess had gone to make sure the extra room was ready for her and Chase while the men were in the barn packing what they'd needed for the trip. Best-case scenario, they'd be home by dark tomorrow night, but she knew that the Duke brothers wouldn't give up without a fight.

A chill ran through her as it started snowing again. Handling the stress was still a challenge most days. She was worried about Chase going in the morning, especially with his recent injuries, but after talking with Margaret, she was also worried about her father. Encountering the

Duke brothers again was going to trigger a slew of emotions that he might not be prepared to handle.

Morgan was standing in the doorway when Hope turned to go back inside.

"Hey. . ." Hope dropped the empty tub to her side. "You okay?"

"Honestly, I'm having a hard time processing. It wasn't even supposed to be a dangerous trip. How did this happen?"

Hope shook her head, wishing she had an answer. "All I know is that they'll do everything in their power to find Jace and bring him back."

Morgan's gaze swept the ground. "Which is why I need to ask you to do a favor for me."

"Of course." The wind shot a shiver through Hope. "But let's go inside."

She followed Morgan into the house then set the empty tub back on the kitchen counter before turning to her sister-in-law.

"I've already talked to Tess," Morgan said, getting straight to the point. "I need the two of you to take care of Noah for me the next couple days."

"Wait. . ." Hope leaned back against the counter. "Why?"

"I'm going with Chase and your father to find my husband."

Hope glanced toward the barn. Her gut response was that Morgan going with them wasn't a good idea, and she had a feeling Chase would agree. "Have you talked to Chase?"

"I don't need his permission to go out searching for my husband."

"I know, but it's not you that I'm worried about. It's Noah." Hope tried to put her thoughts into words. The young boy had already lost one parent when the grid went down and his father was killed in a car accident. "How's he going to react to both you and Jace being gone?"

Morgan shook her head. "Don't tell me you wouldn't do the same thing if you were in my shoes."

Hope's hand went automatically to her stomach. She probably would do the same thing, but life had thrown enough curve balls at her to realize that the answers weren't always black and white, or easy for that matter.

She shook her head. "It's not that I don't think you could keep up with them, or even that you wouldn't be a help, I just think that Noah needs you right now."

Morgan pressed her lips together for a moment. "I understand, and trust me, I've thought through this, but I can't shelter him from what's going on. I haven't been able to since all of this started."

"I know how hard it's been."

Morgan's shoulder's slumped. "You have to understand that when Tommy died, I felt as if my world had ended. I didn't know how I was supposed to be a single mom, let alone survive in this world where everything felt impossible. I woke up with anxiety attacks every morning for months. Worked as hard as I could, motivated only because of Noah. I couldn't lose him, even on the days I wanted to join Tommy and be done with this world."

Hope waited silently for Morgan to continue.

"I was so afraid after Tommy died," Morgan said finally. "I didn't think I could let anybody in, and I was angry at God because I felt like He could've stopped all this." She shook her head. "Sometimes I still think that. I have to keep reminding myself that God is still good. That even though I might not be able to control what others do, or what is happening out there, I can control what's happening in here." She pressed her hand against her heart. "Then Jace came along and changed everything for both of us. Maybe I'm trying to talk myself into going, but the bottom line is that my husband is out there and I need to help find him."

"Okay." Hope nodded, knowing she wasn't going to change Morgan's mind, and besides, this wasn't her decision to make. "What else do you need from me?"

"I'd like to stay here tonight, so I don't have to go back to town. I'd appreciate it. I can work with Margaret to come up with food for the trip, but if I could borrow some warm clothes—"

"Of course. Anything you need." Hope went to the coatrack and grabbed one of her heavier jackets. "I'll come with you to talk to Chase."

Hope had just grabbed her coat when Chase walked into the kitchen.

"I know you both have a lot on your plates," he said, "but we need to take enough food and water for the three of us, and I could use some help."

Hope didn't miss the fatigue in her husband's voice.

"Make that four people," she said, hanging her coat back up. "Morgan wants to go with you, and I think you need to let her go."

"Okay," Chase said.

Morgan took a step forward as if she hadn't heard his answer. "You know what it's like to think you've lost the one important person in your life. And to have to sit back and do nothing. I can't do that. I won't do that. I need to go—"

"Morgan," Chase said. "I said okay."

Morgan blushed as she glanced at Hope then back at Chase. "You did, didn't you."

"You know the area we're going to better than I do. I think you'll be valuable." Chase nodded at Hope. "And somehow, I have a feeling my wife would be doing the exact same thing."

"What's the plan?" Morgan asked.

"The tracks led toward Hangman's Ridge, where it makes sense that the Duke brothers are probably using a cabin. If we cut across the south side of the ranch and head up the ridge we can stop at their mother's place on the way. See if she can tell us anything."

"That narrows it down," Morgan said, "but snowing again, and if we can't follow the tracks, it's a lot of ground to cover. There are dozens of cabins scattered up along that ridge."

Chase frowned. "I can't stop thinking that I should have tried to follow their tracks instead of returning here for help."

"No. You made the right decision," Morgan said. "And I believe Jace would agree with me. Going after them alone would have been too risky. We'll find him."

Chase nodded. They'd find him, because there wasn't another option.

THUNDER CRASHED in the distance an hour later as Hope pulled the thick quilt up around her neck and snuggled against Chase in the cozy queen-sized bed. "I'm worried about your going back out there."

He pulled her closer. "We'll be careful, and I'll be fine. We've been through far worse than this."

He was right, but that didn't make it any easier. If experience had taught her anything, it had showed her the importance of appreciating each moment and finding joy in the small things. For some reason, though, even Chase's nearness wasn't enough to erase the fear tonight.

"I was surprised how quickly you agreed that Morgan could go with you," she whispered in the darkness.

"I meant what I said. I trust her instincts, and know you would have done the same thing."

She let out a soft laugh. "True."

He brushed a strand of her hair off her shoulder. "I wish I didn't have to leave again."

She smiled. "You're reading my thoughts."

"What else are you thinking?" he asked.

She drew in a deep breath, pausing at the question. Her thoughts felt more like a mess of cords she couldn't quite untangle. Layers of stress and concerns that pressed against her heart and made it hard to breathe. Her faith had grown over the past two years as she'd seen God move over and over, but she still found herself falling into that same trap of anxiety.

"I know we've said this before," she said finally. "I'd like to be able to just breathe for a few days without having to deal with any of the mess and the sadness and the pain. Most of the time I feel like I'm simply trying to stay afloat."

"I know this has been hard on you. You've taken on so much."

"Please don't think I'm complaining," she said, moving her hand to his chest. "But sometimes—like today—it's overwhelming."

"I know."

Her mind raced, no matter how hard she tried to slow it down and not worry. She wanted to tell him about the baby, but something stopped her. That would have to wait until they had time to celebrate together without all the distractions—not when her brother was still missing.

Lightning flashed in the distance, as he leaned in and kissed her slowly. "Have I told you recently how grateful I am that you're my wife?"

She grinned. "Just once or twice."

"And I'll be back as soon as I can. I promise."

"You better, but this time please try not to get shot."

Chase laughed, then groaned at the movement. "Don't make me laugh."

"I'm sorry." She frowned, her mind automatically switching to doctor mode. "How are you feeling? It's possible for concussion symptoms not to be obvious for several days, so—"

"I'm fine," he said, kissing her again.

"Chase?"

"Hmm?"

"One more thing before you go to sleep. I'm actually more worried about my father going than Morgan. He's been through so much, and going after the men who shot him...I'm not sure that's a good idea."

"I know things have been hard for him, but you're father's stronger than you think, Hope."

"I know he's strong, but the Duke brothers...they tried to take his life. I don't want him to have to relive that day again. I spoke with Margaret, and she's worried about him. I hadn't really noticed with all the busyness, but he's been distant lately."

"Maybe he just needs some space. The anniversary of your mom's death is just around the corner. Maybe that's a part of it."

"Maybe."

"Plus, he's the best tracker around, and we need him to find Jace." He squeezed her hand. "We'll be careful, I promise. No unnecessary risks. It's going to be okay."

She wanted to believe him, but what if it wasn't okay?

"Will you talk to him for me?" she asked. "Please. Get a feel of where he is and whether or not he should be going."

"If you feel so strongly about him not going, it seems like you should be the one talking to him. Not me. You're his daughter."

"Which is why I don't think he'd listen to me," Hope said. "My father can be. . .stubborn."

"And you think he'll listen to me?"

She nuzzled her head into his shoulder. "He'll think I'm being emotional. He'll think you're looking after the best interest of the team."

"I don't know, Hope. I trust your instincts, but I think you're taking on too much worry—"

"Just. . .feel him out. That's all I'm asking. Make sure he's going into this with his head on straight."

"Okay. I'll talk to him in the morning."

A moment later, she could hear his soft snores coming from beside her. Maybe it was hormones from the pregnancy, but Chase was right. She needed to stop worrying and just trust that somehow, everything was going to be all right.

CHAPTER NINE

Jace woke up to the sound of the men snoring on the other side of the cabin. He rolled over onto his side as quietly as he could while trying to adjust to the darkness. Wyatt was supposed to have taken the first watch, but for the moment, there was no movement. Of course, he knew that trying to escape from the warm cabin at night would be foolish. The temperature had dropped below freezing, and a light snow fell. On top of that, he didn't even know for sure where they were.

But that didn't mean he wasn't going to try.

He worked to break the zip ties against his raw wrists, trying to form a plan, all the while thinking of Morgan. She'd once asked him why it was important for him to protect the town of Shadow Ridge, especially considering the fact that he'd never planned to stay in the town he'd grown up in. It was true he'd never planned to stay in Shadow Ridge. He'd just come for his parents' anniversary, but then, in one fatal weekend, not only had he lost his mother, he'd watched his father change into a man he hardly knew.

The town of Shadow Ridge had been left both without power and the presence of law enforcement. With his father injured and Chase missing, the town had quickly recruited Jace and his younger brother Levi to take over until their father was back on his feet. Every week, Jace had expected it to be over. Expected to be able to head back home across the country to normal. But that had never happened. Instead, he'd found himself investigating murders and thefts while trying to keep the small town safe with no databases, forensic resources, or external experts.

It hadn't been easy, but it had forced him to take a completely different approach to law enforcement and left him struggling with how God would allow so much loss. Past failures he'd made had eaten at him for months until time had slowly begun to change the trajectory of his thoughts. But forgiving himself along with those who'd hurt his family—like the Duke brothers—had been hard.

He hadn't expected to fall in love, but Morgan it made him want to settle down and have a family. Now, not only did he have a wife, he was a father. Noah felt like his own son. And hopefully, one day, they'd bring more children into this world. Morgan was enough to make him grateful he'd stayed.

He weighed his options, but he wasn't going to have another chance like this. Trying to go against all three men while he was unarmed was too risky. But if he could get out of the cabin and away from here, he might have a chance.

He got to his feet as quietly as he could, his hands still

tied in front of him. One of the men stirred from across the room, and Jace froze. Another couple seconds passed, and the rhythmic snoring continued. He slowly made his way across the wooden floor, pausing as one of the boards creaked beneath his weight. Another six feet and he'd be at the door.

He kept moving slowly, trying to assess the risks. He knew that these men would consider murder an option, which upped the risk factor for him, but even that wasn't enough to make him reconsider his decision.

Jace managed to unlock the door with his tethered hands. A gush of wind swept into the room, and he quickly slipped outside and shut the door. It wasn't going to be long until they noticed he was missing. He needed to get as far away, as fast as he could, but he also needed to get out of the zip ties. Halfway across the yard, he raised his hands as high as he could and then in one swift moment, swung his arms toward the ground. The plastic tie snapped in half.

He hurried across the thin layer of snow to the first jeep, hoping his flannel coat was going to be warm enough. He pulled the door open and searched for the key. Nothing. He tried the second jeep. No keys in the second jeep, which meant he was going to have to walk out of here. He decided to take one more look under the passenger seat and hit the jackpot when he pulled out a 9mm Glock.

Now he had a decision to make. He could use the element of surprise and head back into the cabin and try to take the three men down. If he was successful, he could drive out of here with the medicine tonight. But if he wasn't successful. . .

A shout from the cabin made the decision for him.

Three against one weren't odds he wanted to deal with. Not when he knew they'd shoot to kill. He turned around and headed for the dense tree line. Halfway there, his foot got tangled in some sort of trip wire. He managed to keep his balance, but the damage was already done. A string of loud pops followed, alerting the men of the direction he was going.

He ran through the trees as fast as he could, while wondering if he just traded one disaster for another. He wasn't sure what Elijah Duke planned to do with him, but at least inside the cabin he'd been warm. Outside, snow had started to fall again, and the temperature was still dropping. He wasn't going to last long if he didn't find shelter. He knew the area between Alpine and Shadow Ridge fairly well, but finding his way in the dark wasn't going to be easy. He shoved his hands deeper into his pockets and kept moving forward, following the direction of the stars as best he could. He'd learned a lot these last couple years. Things that he used to take for granted had suddenly become essential to staying alive.

He zipped up his flannel coat. There was no way to cover up his tracks and no way to know how long it was going to take him to find shelter, but he'd made the right choice.

Staying would have cost him his life.

"McQuaid, stop where you are, or I'll shoot."

Jace ignored the order and kept running as fast as he could through the darkness. Anger toward the men behind him intensified. His lungs burned from the cold. He ran as far as he could then leaned against the tall trunk of a pine tree, trying to catch his breath while watching for movement behind him. He was tired, cold, and worried about hypothermia almost as much as he was worried about Elijah Duke.

Both could be deadly.

A coyote howled in the distance, but he could no longer hear the rustling of footsteps from behind him. Maybe he'd lost them. Someone shouted from behind him, followed by the sound of a gunshot, proving that theory wrong. Jace picked up his pace again because he knew that if he didn't outrun them, he was about to be the Duke brothers' next victim.

CHAPTER TEN

CHASE WOKE as the first rays of sunlight breached the horizon. His sleep had been peppered with vivid nightmares that left him exhausted, but he needed to get up. He turned over and studied his wife's sleeping form for a moment, wishing he didn't have to leave her again.

Hope rolled over and rested her head on his shoulder. "Good morning. How are you feeling?"

He didn't want to tell her that he'd barely slept. Both from pain and from concern about the situation.

"Definitely better than I was last night," he said.

"I'm glad, but I'm still worried about your going."

"I'll be fine." Chase kissed her forehead. "Why don't you go back to sleep? I know you're tired, and you don't have to get up with us. Sleep another hour."

"No, I need to get you some breakfast," she said, sitting up. "And check your wound—"

"Morgan packed plenty of food for us last night, and you left the pain medicine on the counter. You can redress the wound when I'm back tonight with Jace and the medicine."

"That's very optimistic, thinking you'll be back tonight."

"It is, but that's what I'm praying," he said. "If not, your father can patch me up."

He couldn't read her expression in the semi-darkness, but he knew exactly what she was thinking.

"You were going to talk with my father," she said.

"I know. I haven't forgotten."

"But you think I'm worried about nothing."

"Not at all." He shook his head. "I think this is a very tough situation with a lot of emotions involved and no easy answers. I'll talk to him. I'm just. . . I'm not expecting him to agree with me."

"Just talking to him is enough. Thank you."

"Will you promise to try not to worry in the meantime?" he asked.

"That's probably not going to happen," she said, leaning against him. "Just come back to me soon."

"That's my plan. Now go to back sleep."

He was surprised but thankful when she laid down again. He pulled the quilt up around her shoulders, watching her for another moment before he got out of bed. His side ached at the movement, and he was already dreading getting back on a horse. A least his head didn't hurt and, while he was tired, he didn't feel as groggy as he had last night.

He shivered as he picked up the shirt he'd laid out the night before and buttoned it up in the darkness. He was still questioning their plan as he headed out of the bedroom, wondering if it was foolish not to consider bringing in a few more men to track down the Duke brothers. But he also knew that security both in town and the outlying areas were already stretched thin. No. They'd stick with their plan and return with a larger group only if absolutely necessary.

Kellan and Morgan were already drinking coffee in the kitchen when he stepped into the room. The temperature had dropped overnight, and a glance outside the window showed a deeper layer of snow across the ground than there had been last night.

"How are you feeling?" Kellan asked.

"Achy, but better." Chase touched his side before pouring himself some coffee.

"I thought of something last night," Garret said, walking into the room.

Chase turned to his father-in-law, his conversation with Hope still in the forefront of his mind. He understood Hope's concerns, but he also knew that they needed his father-in-law. Not only was he an expert tracker, he knew the Duke brothers better than anyone else.

"We need to talk to Elijah and Adam's mother," Garrett said. "Nellie Duke still lives in the direction of Hangman's Ridge. According to her, they don't come around often, but if they're nearby, they might go see her."

"Makes sense," Chase said. "We could stop there on our way up to the ridge."

"You think she might know where they are?" Morgan asked.

Garrett nodded. "If they're nearby, I think it's very possible."

"What do you know about her?" Chase asked, leaning against the counter.

"She lives alone and rarely comes into town. I'm pretty sure her sons bring her supplies every few months. She's never denied seeing them, but she claims they never tell her where they've been or where they're going."

"The more information we have going after them the better," Chase said, downing a dose of the white bark tincture for pain Hope left on the counter for him. He winced at the bitterness. "I think it's a good idea."

Chase had always respected his father-in-law's opinions. The older man might have spent most of his law enforcement career dealing with the mundane issues of a small town, but his integrity and his dedication to protect this area had always made him a hero in Chase's mind.

Jace once told him that Garrett McQuaid had been born in the wrong century, and during the months he'd worked with him, Chase had discovered it was true. Garrett had never had much use for technology and social media, preferring instead the stark simplicity and silence the backcountry and desert offered. But despite his numerous roles of chief of police, EMT, educator, and counselor, the man was a family man at heart. Which was why suggesting he might want to reconsider going after his son probably wasn't going to go over well.

"I'll saddle up the horses," Kellan said.

"I'm ready and can help," Morgan said.

Chase turned to Garrett, wanting to respect his wife's request without overstepping a line. "Can I talk to you for a moment before we go out?"

"Of course."

"We'll be out in a minute." Chase waited for Kellan and Morgan to head outside before turning back to Garrett. "I just want to make sure you're okay going with us. I know that hunting down the Duke brothers is personal—"

"I've been looking for the man who shot me for almost two years, and now they have my son," Garrett said. "So you bet this is personal."

Chase studied the older man's expression. "Too personal for you to be involved in the search?"

Garrett took a step back at the question. "You think I should stay behind?"

"That's not my call to make—"

"No, but you're worried that I might turn this into some kind of revenge mission."

Chase searched for the right words. "I've never known you to be that kind of person, but that said, I know how hard it's been."

He tried to read Garrett's expression but could only see pain. Pain he was sure came with a flood of memories. The man had lost a lot.

"I know you're worried about Jace—" Chase said, suddenly wishing that he'd stayed out of this.

"Jace is why I need to go," Garrett said, dropping his hands to his sides. "Jace and Margaret. She needs that medicine. But if you don't think I'm capable of pulling my weight—"

"It's not that at all, I just—"

"Hope told you to talk to me, didn't she?" Garrett grabbed his hat off the table. "She's worried about me going out there."

There was no use trying to deny the truth. "She loves you, and yes, she's worried."

"I know she's just trying to protect me, but I've been doing this a lot longer than she's even been alive. I won't deny it's personal, but I know how to separate my emotions from my job."

"I understand." Chase hesitated before moving forward with his train of thought. "Honestly, I think this situation has triggered a lot of memories for Hope. I'm not sure she's completely dealt with her grief. She was there when they brought you to the clinic after you'd been shot. She was there right after her mother died."

Garrett tapped his hat against his leg. "I was in and out of consciousness and don't even remember those first few days after the grid went down, but I know it was hard for her."

"I've always regretted not being here for you and Hope, especially after you lost Kat."

Garrett shook his head. "I'm the one who's always regretted sending you off on that prisoner transfer. If I hadn't, you would have been here with Hope all that time."

"Neither of us could have anticipated what happened."

Or how that day would change so much for everyone.

Chase knew about the depression that had lingered after his father-in-law's injury, and how it had taken months until he'd been able to return to work.

"I guess I can't blame her for worrying about me." Garrett gazed past Chase as if he were suddenly lost in the past. "When I went out that day to look for the Duke brothers, I promised Kat I'd be back in plenty of time for us to celebrate our anniversary. I never imagined I'd have to bury her instead."

Chase understood. The destruction across the country had changed everything.

"Stop worrying about me," Garrett said, shaking his

head. "You have enough on your plate. I'll be fine. And we will find Jace and the medicine."

"Yes, sir."

"I think deep down Hope understands this is something I need to do. Both for Jace, and yes, for myself."

Chase nodded, not willing to push the conversation any further. "Then let's go find your son."

By the time they headed out on horseback, the sun had slid above the horizon. Chase hung back at the rear, praying for wisdom and safety, as Garrett took the lead. Traveling at night was avoided unless it was an emergency, but traveling in the daylight could be just as dangerous, as bandits made attempts to take advantage of vulnerable travelers.

But a possible ambush was only one of the things worrying him.

Chase looked out across the white ground cover as they road south across the ranchland. This part of the state had unpredictable weather, and with no Weather Channel for updates, a winter storm could quickly take them by surprise. And while blizzard conditions and heavy snow had always made travel conditions difficult, making the trip by horseback brought with it added risks.

He shifted his gaze to Morgan, who worried him as well. It wasn't that he didn't trust her or believe that she wouldn't hold her own, but he knew Jace would never forgive him for putting her in a dangerous situation if something went wrong.

Which was why all he could do at this point was pray that he'd made the right decisions and do everything he could to find his brother-in-law.

CHAPTER ELEVEN

GARRETT PULLED up the collar of his coat as they rode away from the ranch headed south toward the ridge, praying he was right. Maybe he should have stayed behind like Chase had implied, because while the nightmares had finally disappeared for the most part, there wasn't a day he didn't wake up missing Kat or notice she wasn't lying in the bed beside him.

To this day, he was still haunted by the realization that she wasn't coming back.

Memories of Kat continued to surface, unwanted. They'd married when he was only nineteen, and when she died forty years later, he'd felt as if he'd lost his entire identity. Even another four decades together with his first love in this quiet part of the state wouldn't have been enough.

His gaze took in the surrounding terrain as they continued riding at a steady pace. The snow had stopped falling, but not before accumulating a good two inches. Despite all that had happened, he still loved it out here, surrounded by orchards, pine trees, and the unique combination of both the desert and forested mountains. Living just outside the small town of Shadow Ridge had been all he and Kat ever knew. It had also been all they'd ever wanted. They'd had five children, and he'd always pictured himself and Kat growing old together with their grandchildren. Katherine held the family together with phone calls, Sunday lunches after church, and holiday gatherings, while he'd worked to keep the town and surrounding area as safe as possible.

And then in one moment, he'd lost everything.

He shifted in the saddle. It had taken him a long time to feel normal again—if normal was even an option in this world. He'd lost not only his ability to walk for a season, but also his ability to fight. Losing his mobility had left him feeling worthless. With his sons taking over his job, he'd realized that they didn't need him. The town didn't need him.

And then there was Margaret.

Margaret had been Kat's best friend for as long as he could remember. After Kat died, she became his physical therapist, and for months that's all their relationship had been. As a retired nurse, she'd done the impossible by making him get up every day for physical therapy, and he hadn't gone easy on her. For months, he never thought for even a moment of moving on to a new relationship, especially if it meant falling in love again. He didn't need anyone else. After forty years, Kat had given him enough love and security to last a lifetime.

He wasn't even sure when he first noticed the change in his feelings. He started looking forward to Margaret coming over. After his sessions, they'd end up drinking coffee on the veranda and talking for hours. She was the one who made him laugh again. She was also the one who had no problem putting him in his place when he needed it.

But even after all this time, he couldn't shake Kat.

He hadn't wanted to admit to Chase that something was wrong, but Hope was right. He wasn't sure what was holding him back from moving forward with Margaret. It wasn't that he was worried about what his children would think, or even the town. Maybe it was the fact that after so much loss, he was terrified of loving—and then losing again. He'd never been a man to give in to fear, but thoughts of a relationship had him wanting to run the opposite direction.

A grackle clacked in a tree to his left, pulling him out of his turbulent thoughts. The trail they were on narrowed slightly as it turned southeast and started up an incline.

"It's just another half a mile, then we'll take a side road to the house," Garrett said.

"You weren't kidding when you said she lived off the beaten path," Morgan said.

"Honestly, I'm not sure how she's managed to survive out here on her own."

The temperature continued to drop by the time they got to the short dirt road that led up to the familiar casita that was halfway between town and Hangman's Ridge. He'd been here more than once in an attempt to track down the men who'd shot him. At first, he'd come simply to track down the brothers, but he hadn't been able to forget what he'd found. Before the grid went down, Nellie Duke had lived off social security and disability. After the grid went down, like thousands of other people, she'd found herself cut off from those crucial resources.

Garrett dismounted. "I think it'll be best if I go in alone. I can't say that she trusts me, but I have managed to build a rapport with her."

"You sure?" Chase asked.

Garrett nodded, took the food packet they'd put together from Morgan, and headed up to the house by himself. A moment later, he stopped on the porch and knocked on the door.

"Nellie?"

A moment later, she opened the door with a rifle in her hand.

"Garrett McQuaid," she said. "It's been a while."

"How are you, Nellie?" Garrett asked, genuinely wanting to know.

"Still alive, as if that matters."

"I'd like to come in and talk to you," he said, holding up the fresh bread and some winter vegetables. It's not much, but we thought it might help."

"We?" she asked, looking past him.

"My two sons-in-law and my daughter-in-law," Garrett said.

"You always had a big family. Garrett McQuaid and his boys, running this town like royalty."

"Just trying to keep the town safe," Garrett said, ignoring the comment.

"From my side, it looks as if you've done quite well, unlike some of us."

Garrett started to throw out a sharp comeback then stopped when he read the pain in the woman's eyes. Just like he'd never expected to be a widower, she'd never expected to live on her own or watch her boys grow up to be felons.

"I just want to talk," Garrett repeated.

"Fine. Come on in."

The small room was dark, with only a little light coming in through the window. No family photos hung on the walls or on the mantel. Just a few dusty paintings and knickknacks. No sign of her sons.

Garrett sat down on the couch. "I'll get straight to the point. We need to find Elijah and Adam."

Nellie laughed as she sat down in the worn recliner across from him. "Good luck with that. Nothing's changed since the last time I saw you. I haven't seen them for months."

"Your boys held up a train and stole a bunch of medical supplies," Garrett said.

Nellie's solemn expression didn't change. "Like I told you, I haven't seen them for months."

Garrett leaned forward. "They also kidnapped my oldest son."

"I'm sorry." This time she frowned, but there was no compassion in her voice as she said, "But that doesn't change the fact that I haven't seen them."

Garrett searched for a way to approach the woman. "Nellie. . .there are people's lives at stake here. I need you to give me something. We believe they're staying nearby. Possibly on the south side of the ridge. Where would they go if they needed a place to lay low?"

"Not to their mother's, obviously."

Garrett frowned at the confession. His family wasn't perfect, but they were family. Something Nellie probably never had.

Nellie flicked a crumb off the arm of her chair, this

time avoiding his gaze. "Why do you keep checking on me and bringing me food?"

"I know you're alone," Garrett said, surprised at her question. "And I know things have to be hard for you."

"I don't understand." She let out a low laugh. "I'm not naive. My son shot you and left you for dead. Both of them deserve to be behind bars. I'm their mother, and I'll be the first to admit it."

"You're not the one who pulled the trigger," Garrett said.

"Do you know what it's like to be betrayed by family?"

He hesitated with his response. "I know what it's like to be betrayed."

"My husband left me when the boys were little. I took on extra jobs, tried to keep some sense of normalcy. . . I know it all sounds like a boatload of excuses. I made mistakes, but I never had the support of a family like you have."

"I'm sorry. I know it couldn't have been easy."

Nellie stared past him for a few long seconds. "Why do you care what happens to me?"

"Because you're a part of this community."

"Am I? I have a feeling you're not bringing those food packets to the entire town."

"No, but I've spent enough time on my knees with my heavenly Father to realize that once I allow bitterness in, it'll take over and consume me. It's not easy, but I don't want that to happen."

She glanced back at the table. "So this is a form of penance?"

Her question surprised him. "No, not penance. I'm just trying to do what's right."

"You always were a puzzle to me, Garret McQuaid." She leaned back in the recliner. "There might be a place. Elijah mentioned it the last time he was here. A cabin that belonged to a friend of his. Matt. . .no. . .Max Weatherly, I think was his name. It's pretty remote, with lots of tree covering. Not a place conducive to growing food, but definitely a place to hide."

"Where is it?" Garrett asked.

"I don't know exactly. From what I remember, it was five or six miles up the ridge from here, past Danby Trail."

Garrett nodded. It was definitely possible, as the directions fit what Chase told him.

"Thank you, Nellie."

She shrugged. "I'd just hate to think that they're that close and didn't come to see me."

Garrett stood up. "If you need anything, I can connect you with resources in town."

"You've told me that before, but I'm not interested in religion."

"This isn't about religion," he said, opening the door and stepping out onto the porch. "It's about community and, for me, trying to follow a relationship with my creator."

"Maybe if your God had stepped in back then, you wouldn't be knocking on my door today."

Garrett stood on the porch as Nellie shut the door, wishing he had a better answer for the woman. Wondering what that answer would have been. Wondering if she would have listened if he'd said the right thing.

Kat would have known what to say.

Shaking off the reproach, he quickly gave the others an

update of his conversation with Nellie as he headed toward his horse.

"I know that place," Morgan said, when he'd finished. "Max Weatherly used to come down to the café every month, but I haven't seen him since the grid went down."

"Can you take us there?" Chase asked.

"Between Nellie's directions and my memory of the place...yes. I think so."

"Good," Garrett said.

"And if Jace isn't there?" she asked.

Garrett turned and caught his daughter-in-law's gaze. "We're going to find him. Wherever he is."

CHAPTER TWELVE

MORGAN URGED her horse to pick up the pace as they rode toward Max Weatherly's cabin. She didn't know much about the man except that he'd seemed to be somewhat of a loner despite being a regular at her café before the grid went down. She also knew he'd had a few brushes with the law, which made a connection with the Duke brothers plausible.

She'd been surprised at how Chase hadn't questioned her decision to come with them, but then again, they'd all had to do things out of their comfort zone. Most of it hadn't come easy for her, and it wasn't just the fact that Tommy's death had left her a widow and a single mom. In an instant, everything normal had vanished. With no deliveries or resources, she'd had to close the diner. There hadn't even been time to properly grieve for those they'd lost. The town had buried their dead then immediately switched to survival mode.

Hours had quickly turned into days, which turned into

weeks, with no end in sight. Months of living on the edge left her exhausted most days and always second-guessing her parenting skills of an overly adventurous boy who'd lost his father. No electricity or clean water made daily chores challenging. She'd gone from running the town's diner to taking over her husband's greenhouses, raising rabbits and chickens, and learning how to preserve a harvest without electricity. All in order to feed her child and survive.

Jace was the unexpected piece of the puzzle she'd never anticipated. In fact, neither of them had expected their relationship to go beyond friendship. She'd recently lost her husband and had a child to raise, and Jace had a town to protect. But somehow, they'd found each other and that surprise spark had turned to love.

She ran her thumb across the back of her wedding ring. She'd always miss Tommy, but she and Jace had gone through so much together. She wasn't going to lose her husband.

Not now.

Not this way.

The cold wind whipped through the collar of her thick jacket, sending chills down her spine as they rode the trail through a grove of trees. She wasn't the same person she'd been before the grid went down. None of them were. The loss of everything they'd known guaranteed that. For so long, she'd taken things for granted. Hot showers. Cell phone service. Air-conditioning. . . And yet, even on the hardest days, she was learning to be grateful. Unexpectedly, Jace had been a part of that process.

In the end, marriage wasn't easy. Parenting wasn't easy. Especially when there was so much on the line every day just to survive. But despite the difficult road they were on, Jace had managed to help her find balance and live her life to the fullest. It was something she hoped she never stopped doing. Something she wanted to keep striving for with Jace until they were old and gray.

"I need him back, Jesus." Her voice was barely a whisper as she spoke the words out loud and fought back the tears.

She hadn't cried since receiving the news that Jace had been kidnapped. Instead, she'd finally managed to fall asleep last night, exhausted and barely able to process what happened. She'd also wanted to be strong for Noah, which meant telling her son that his father had been delayed, but they were going to pray that he'd be back soon. Not the entire truth, but not a lie either.

She'd also meant what she'd said to Hope, but that didn't stop the hundred what-ifs as she second-guessed her decision to join Chase and Garrett.

Her mind was still processing the situation when something on the ground caught her eye. She pulled back on the reins and brought the mare to a stop. "Hang on, I think I found something."

Chase turned around. "You okay?"

She nodded, then jumped off her horse and headed toward one of the trees where she'd caught the flash of orange. It was probably nothing. Just her desperation to find Jace. She picked up the small piece of fabric and recognized the pattern of Jace's brown and orange flannel coat he'd taken with him on the trip.

"Jace has a coat like this," she said, holding up the piece of fabric.

Chase nodded. "He was wearing it on the train."

"Then he's out here somewhere," Morgan said.

Chase dismounted and walked toward her while she looked for footprints, but most of the ground was covered with a fresh layer of snow.

"How far away do you think we are from the cabin?" Garrett asked, joining them.

Morgan stood back up. "A half a mile. Maybe a bit more."

"Hold on," Garrett said, squatting about six feet from her. "I just found something else."

Morgan hurried over then crouched down next to him, the snippet of flannel still in her hands. Her heart plummeted when she saw the dots of dark blood against the thin layer of white snow.

"We can't assume anything," he said, looking up at her. "We have no idea whose blood this is, but it's recent."

"He's right," Chase said.

Morgan tried to squelch the panic, but it wasn't possible. "If he's been injured. . ."

Or if he's by himself, or dying.

What did they do to him?

She pressed back the negative thoughts and instead tried working through a different scenario. If he'd escaped, he would have tried to head to Shadow Ridge for help. But if that was true, wouldn't they have already found him? Maybe the men were stalking him and he'd taken another trail to avoid being found. But either way, if he was injured, they needed to find him.

"This is the most used trail," she said. "Over the last couple of years, it's been worn by horses, making a straight shot from the top of the ridge back down to town, but it's not the only trail up the ridge." Morgan turned to the men, her mind racing. "Jace knows this area pretty well. If someone was after him, he might have left the main trail and headed through the trees to pick up the secondary one west of here."

"That makes sense," Kellan said.

Garrett held up his hand, interrupting the conversation.

"Kellan. . .Morgan. . .Chase. . . Don't move."

Morgan saw what her father-in-law was looking at a moment after he did.

Twenty yards away were two coyotes. Both were thin and looked hungry. Morgan's heart pounded as one of them let out a long, eerie howl. She took a step back toward her horse, afraid it might bolt, then saw a third and forth one. A shiver ran down her spine as the one to the left of where she stood started toward her, seemingly unafraid.

"Morgan, don't move. Just stay where you are, facing him."

"They're circling," she said, trying to keep the panic out of her voice.

"I know."

The howling grew. So did her fear.

She pressed her hand against her chest, her heart pounding. She knew that fatal coyote attacks on humans were rare, but just six weeks ago, a twenty-year-old woman back in Shadow Ridge had been attacked and later died. Competing heavily with humans for food sources from the wild had led to conflicts that normally wouldn't have happened. These canines were clever and ate pretty much anything, and now they'd become fearless.

Chase raised his handgun and fired a shot into the air.

The coyotes barely flinched. He fired another one, and they finally ran away, disappearing moments later into the trees.

"Are you okay?" Garrett asked, running up to her.

She nodded, irritated at how rattled the encounter had left her. "I just want to find Jace."

Morgan pressed down the fear and mounted her horse. She was cold and tired and, from the dark skies, it looked like another storm was brewing on the horizon. They had enough food and water for a couple of days, as well as tents and warm sleeping bags, but she wasn't worried about those things. She was worried about the men they were more than likely about to encounter.

The men who had her husband.

"We're going to need to be extra careful from here on out," Garrett said, taking the lead. "They're not going to let anyone just walk onto the property without them knowing."

"What do you mean?" Morgan asked.

"They'll either have someone standing guard, or have set up some kind of trip wire," Chase answered.

Morgan frowned. More and more people back in town had done the same thing, after realizing that home defense was essential. Not for the first time, she wondered if maybe Hope was right. Maybe she should have stayed back in Shadow Ridge. She had a son who needed Jace, but he also needed his mother, and being out here was risky.

They weren't dealing with someone who just wanted to keep their home safe from intruders. They were looking at men who had no qualms about getting rid of anyone who got in their way. From everything she knew about these men, they wouldn't hesitate to set a booby trap designed to not only to stop an intruder, but to injure or kill them.

And whatever trap was ahead, if they weren't careful, they were about to walk right into it.

CHAPTER THIRTEEN

Hope stomped the snow off her boots before stepping into the ranch house. It had been a long morning at the clinic, and while part of her wished she'd gone with Chase, she knew she needed to stay. Of course, that had been the story of her life the last two years. So many people needing her. So many impossible situations she'd been thrust into. It was always the waiting that was the hardest. Waiting with no way to communicate and let her know that he was okay.

She hung her damp coat on the rack by the door then sat down on the coffee table in order to warm up by the fire.

"I didn't expect you back so early," Tess said, walking into the room.

"Hey. . ." Hope smiled up at her sister. "Things were actually quiet at the clinic, so I left Karen and Mrs. Carlson in charge. I thought I'd come back to check on Margaret and see if you needed help with Noah. I just need a minute to warm up."

"He's been an angel, actually. He's in with Margaret. She's reading him Narnia, his new favorite series from the library."

The thought of the Narnia series brought with it a rush of nostalgia. "I loved it when Dad read those stories to us."

"Me too." Tess smiled, sitting down on the edge of the coffee table. "I don't think the boys appreciated them as much as we did, but I've read them at least twice since then."

A screeching noise jarred Hope's attention. She turned toward the front door. "What was that?"

Tess jumped up. "It's my egg-thief alarm."

"Wait. . . Your what?"

Tess grabbed her coat off the rack. "I made a trap and rigged it with one of those self-defense sirens."

Hope's mind was still back at the thief part of the conversation. "Has someone been stealing your eggs?"

Tess was already out the door.

"Wait up." Hope grabbed her own coat then hurried outside into the cold. She finally caught up with her sister in front of the barn.

Tess paused at the door. "Something's been stealing the eggs. We actually think it might be one of the barn cats, helping itself to a midnight snack. Whatever it is, with winter egg production already way down, we can't afford to lose any."

Hope whacked the flashlight as it glitched. No. . .no. . .no. . .With an overcast sky, it was going to be dark inside the barn, and this was not the time for the battery to go out. But as serious as the situation was, somehow the thought of her artistic sister building a trap and trying to catch an egg thief made Hope want to chuckle.

"Did you ever imagine the two of us, both married to lawmen, out trying to catch an egg thief?" Hope asked.

"Straight out of the wild west and one of Dad's Louis L'Amour books."

"Or like we're Rizzoli and Isles," Hope said, "about to take down a criminal."

"As long as I'm Rizzoli. I've learned I don't do well with dead bodies." Tess laughed. "Honestly, I've always been happy to let our husbands do the crime-solving heroics, but when it comes to my chickens. . .I'm out for revenge."

Hope held up the flashlight then opened the door slowly while Tess aimed her handgun in front of her.

"Watch your aim," Hope said, only half joking.

Another loud screech told her that something was inside, and it didn't sound like a barn cat. Other than her dying flashlight, it was dark inside the barn. She aimed it into the shadows.

"Where's the trap?" Hope asked.

"To the left." Tess blew out a sharp breath. "It's empty. How did it set off the alarm without getting caught?"

Another loud noise shifted Hope's attention—and flashlight—to the barn wall. An elongated shadow that looked like some medieval gargoyle appeared. "What in the world. . ."

Hope screamed as the creature flew at her, landing on her chest while barking and whistling. She dropped the flashlight and tried to pull the animal off her as she stumbled backward and out through the open barn door.

"Tess!"

A second later, Hope fell into the water trough. The ice cold water took her breath away.

"Hope?" Tess helped get her out of the water.

"I'm fine. Where is it?"

"I don't know," Tess said, her attention completely on Hope. "Are you okay?"

"Did you see what it was?"

Tess didn't move.

"Tess?" Hope tried to read her sister's reaction. "Am I bleeding?"

"No. I don't think so."

Tess pressed her hand against her mouth.

"Then what?"

"It was a squirrel," her sister finally said, picking up the flickering flashlight.

"A what?"

"A squirrel."

"That's not possible. It was big and it screamed like some. . .some rabid hyena."

"It was a squirrel, Hope." Tess shone the flashlight at her. "No blood. No marks. And I don't think it was rabid, though I do know a good doctor."

Hope looked down at her shirt and frowned. Tess had to be kidding, but there wasn't a mark on her shirt. So that hadn't been some giant, rabid rodent? Just a small squirrel.

Hope started toward the house, her heart still racing. "This. . .this entire incident will never be spoken of again. Never, Tess. Do you understand?"

Tess was still trying not to laugh. "What am I supposed to tell Kellan?"

"That you discovered a squirrel was stealing the eggs. That's all you have to say."

Ten minutes later, Hope had changed out of her wet clothes and was huddled in front of the living room fire on the rug. Tess added a couple more logs then sat down next to her.

"I really am so sorry," her sister said.

Hope squeezed her eyes shut for a moment. "This wasn't your fault, and. . .and I might have overreacted a bit."

"Well, you were attacked by a squirrel that could have been rabid."

This time Hope laughed. "Somehow, I don't think he was rabid."

"He got away."

"But now you know what it is." Hope stared into the fire. "Life really hasn't exactly turned out how I imagined."

"You mean the whole 2.5 kids, a white picket fence, and access to Starbucks and TJ Maxx?"

"Well. . ." Hope shivered. "That and the fact that I just fell into the goat's water trough."

"I shouldn't have laughed."

She shot Tess a smile. "You can be assured that I would have done the same thing if our roles had been reversed."

And yet it was really a reminder of how much things had changed.

How much she'd changed.

When she'd left for school well over a decade ago, she'd promised herself she wouldn't return to the isolated town in the middle of west Texas except to visit. Shadow Ridge had seemed far too small with no malls, no delivery options, and no airport. She'd never wanted to grow old in a little slice of Mayberry. Instead, she wanted her choice of takeout, multiple shopping centers, sports arenas, and coffee shops. And, most of all, she'd wanted to work in a bustling hospital where resources for her patients were extensive, and there was potential for promotion and an actual benefit package that came with the job.

Fast forward to now. She'd learned to use a sidearm, could pluck a chicken for Sunday dinner, make her own homemade soap, and wash clothes without any appliances among a myriad of other skills life had made necessary.

"What are you looking forward to doing after the lights come back on?" Hope asked, still shivering.

"Noah told me this morning that after reading *The Lion, the Witch, and the Wardrobe*, he's excited about Christmas lights coming back on."

Hope laughed. "And you? What are you excited about?"

"I kind of agree with him, but I'd also like to finish school eventually. I've even thought of going back and studying forensic art. As hard as it's been, I've felt a sense of purpose helping Jace and the department with my crime-scene and composite sketches."

"I think you'd do amazing. You've already helped out so much."

Tess had only finished a semester of art school when the grid went down. She'd been the free spirit of the family. A risk-taker who'd always been content to march to her own drum. Losing her mother at nineteen along with everything else that happened had been difficult. When Jace asked Tess to sketch her first crime scene, Hope had feared the work was going to further traumatize Tess.

But, just as with the rest of them, circumstances had changed Tess. She'd found a new confidence, and it translated into her artwork. Then Mr. O'Connor from town had reopened his late wife's studio, allowing Tess to start the art school in town and continue her own creative pursuits as well.

"Do you think things will ever be normal again? Even if the lights do come on?" Tess asked.

"I'm not sure it will ever be the same. Not in the sense of normal we were used to."

Funny. She hardly remember what normal felt like. There had been a time when she hadn't thought twice about ordering take-out on a busy evening, or taking a couple hours to shop for high heels for an outfit. Where a day off meant sitting in a coffee shop for a couple hours, listening to music and catching up on her emails.

Back then, she'd been told she was foolish for leaving her life in the city. That working in a small-town clinic was going to be more like working in a war zone compared to the state-of-the-art, world-class hospital she could be working at. And instead of specializing, she'd be working to treat everything from diabetes to snake bites to delivering babies, and she'd always be on call.

The grid going down had taken things to an entirely different level, leaving her scrambling to deal with things they'd barely touched on in medical school, like cholera, cyanide poisoning, and now, brucellosis. Scouring old textbooks in the town's library had helped, but for the most part she was left to improvise.

"I don't think about it a lot, but there are so many things I can't help but wonder if I'll ever experience," Tess said. "Like college and traveling. Everything is just so different now, and I don't think things will ever go back to the way they were."

"You did find Kellan."

"Which makes all of this worth it." Tess smiled, but

her grin quickly faded. "I'm worried about them. I was hoping they'd be back by now."

"I know. Me too."

A knock on the front door pulled Hope away from the conversation. "Were you expecting someone?"

Tess shook her head then picked up her sidearm before heading to the door.

Hope stood up as their brother Levi's wife stepped into the house.

"Karen told me you were here. It's Josie." Ava pressed her lips together. "She's really sick, and I don't know what to do."

CHAPTER FOURTEEN

Chapter Fourteen

Garrett took the lead as they left the horses behind and approached the cabin on foot, looking for any signs of a booby trap in case Elijah and Adam were here. Most people who used DIY trip wires utilized them not for lethal force, but to scare away people and animals by sounding an alarm that something was approaching.

But the Duke brothers didn't fit the category of *most people*.

Garrett stopped. He knew them well enough to know that they wouldn't hesitate to use lethal force, which put his nerves on edge. He'd used trip wires himself a time or two, including the time he caught two fugitives who couldn't resist the jerrycan of fuel he'd used for bait. But his traps never caused any bodily harm.

"Is everything okay?" Chase said, walking up to him.

"Yeah. I'm going to need a thin two-foot-long branch."

Garrett made sure the safety was on his gun then set it

down for a moment while he dug into his backpack for a length of bright orange paracord.

"What's this for," Chase asked, handing Garrett the requested item a moment later.

"I'm about to make a trip wire detector. More are set about six inches to a foot off the ground."

High enough that someone couldn't just step over the wire without tripping it, and that random rodents won't repeatedly set it off.

A minute later he was walking slowly up the trail, his sidearm held steady in front of him in one hand while in his other hand he carried the branch with the paracord hanging off the end. Another twenty feet, and the dangling cord stopped on a wire. He held up his hand, signaling the others to stop.

"Hold on, we've got our first alarm."

Without his DIY detector he might have missed it. An invisible "doorbell" to alert the homeowner of any intruders. In this case, to alert the Duke brothers that someone was approaching. He leaned over to study what he'd found. The fishing line had been set about twelve inches above the ground and was attached to a grenade head. It wasn't deadly if set off, but the loud *bang* would definitely get someone's attention.

"That's a pretty good sign they're here," Chase said.

"Agreed." Garrett stood back up and continued along the ravine toward the cabin. "Let's keep moving, but be careful. I doubt this is their only defense."

He stopped again as the sunlight reflected ahead off something metal. It had to be the jeeps.

"Go slow," he warned. "They're close."

He skirted the tree line until he could see the vehicles parked twenty feet from the cabin.

"Garrett..." Morgan walked past him. "It's Jace's ball cap."

"Morgan, don't—"

A loud bang like a gunshot went off as she picked up the booby-trapped cap that must have been set with another grenade head.

"Are you okay?" he asked.

She dropped the hat as she stumbled backward, her hands shaking. "I'm so, so sorry."

"It's okay."

Kellan knelt down in front of the trip alarm. "Another grenade head."

"Definitely not lethal," Chase said, "but it still sounds like a gunshot."

The perfect alarm.

Which meant they'd just walked into a trap.

Elijah Duke appeared on the porch, aiming his rifle at them. His brother, along with another armed man, flanked them almost immediately, blocking any escape.

"Garrett McQuaid." Elijah grinned as he walked down the porch stairs. "It's been a long time since I saw you. In fact, I'm a bit surprised to see you're alive, though I heard you've been looking for me."

Garrett held his gun steady at the man. "Apparently God had something else in store for me."

"I'll give you credit. You're good, but not quite good enough. Because clearly my brother and I have managed to evade you until now."

"Enough of the happy reunion," Garrett said. "I'm here to get my son and the medicine."

"It doesn't seem to me that you're in the position to make demands."

"I'm not so sure about that."

"Granted it's four against three, but there are a few things about this place that you don't know about. You don't really think we'd let anyone get this close without us being prepared, do you?"

Elijah let out a deep laugh. The man might be bluffing, but then again...He might be telling the truth. And there was too much at stake here to guess wrong.

Garrett looked around slowly. What was he missing?

"This isn't a game, Elijah," he said. "People's lives are on the line."

Elijah laughed again. "You really don't know me, do you? Not if you think that appealing to my humanity will make me change my mind. You see, there are winners and losers in this mess, and I plan on taking advantage of the situation and win again."

"You won't win," Garrett said.

"Really? That's where you're wrong. There's turmoil across this country, which means plenty of opportunity for us." Elijah was still grinning.

"And my son?" Garrett countered. "Was he a part of the plan?"

"Your son was just a bonus."

"Then where is he?"

"Oh, he tried to run, but let's just say his escape was short lived," Elijah said. "This really is my lucky day. The day we take down Garrett and Jace McQuaid along with all your minions."

"Where is he, Elijah?"

"I'm the one in charge, and here is what's going to happen." Elijah held up his gun.

The sound of a gunshot interrupted Elijah's threats, knocking the weapon from his hand and shifting the balance of power. Someone shouted as Elijah collapsed to the ground. Garrett glanced back as Kellan and Chase took advantage of the distraction and secured the other two men. Then he turned back to Elijah.

"You better not move," Garrett said, standing over the man, his gun aimed at his chest. He wasn't sure who'd made the shot, but it didn't matter. Elijah Duke was finished.

Elijah grabbed his arm and groaned. "I've been shot."

Garrett glanced at the wound. "That's barely a graze. Unfortunately, you'll live."

Something snapped at the words, opening the dam he'd held back for so long. Emotions flooded through him, bringing with them a range of both anger and revenge.

"You don't get it. You ruined my life, and I'm not the only one. How many people have you hurt? Have you ever stopped to think about it? Ever stop for a moment to think about the lives you've ruined by your greed? Your victims. . .their families. . .your mother. If I would have stayed in town with my wife instead of looking for you, she'd still be alive right now. We'd still be together, but you. . .you—"

"Garrett. . ." Chase's voice tried to reach him. "This isn't the place or the time."

"Now is as good a time as any. These men don't deserve my mercy or grace."

"Garrett, put the gun down. They'll be tried as criminals and receive what's due them, but not here. Not this way."

Anger swelled. "Why should I wait for justice to take its course? The rule of law isn't working in this state, let alone the country, which means we might as well handle this ourselves."

"We'll send them to the salt mines and let them pay for their crimes."

Garrett ignored him. "That's not enough. Not when I've waited two years to see the look in his eyes I'm seeing right now. Defeat. Loss. Fear." He sneered at Elijah. "It doesn't feel good, does it? Knowing your life is about to end."

"Shoot me, then," Elijah challenged. "But I know you won't. You don't have the guts to pull the trigger. You always were a coward."

Garrett shook his head. "I'm not the coward here. You're the ones always on the run. Taking what's not yours. Leaving lives in shambles. You don't deserve to live. None of you do."

"All words. You really are a coward."

"Don't listen to him, Garrett. He's not worth you losing your soul."

Garrett didn't move, the barrel of his weapon still rested inches from Elijah's heart. He tried to shove back the memories, but they just came at him faster, one after another. The day he'd encountered Elijah near Crawley's point. Alone, with no backup. The crack of the rifle. The dust blowing across his face as he fell backward onto the ground, unable to move. Barely breathing, he'd felt something wet spreading across his chest and had known at that moment he was going to die in the desert he'd always loved.

He hadn't been able to move, but he remembered a face blurring above him that day.

Jace.

Garrett shifted his attention from Elijah.

Jace was standing next to him. "Dad, I need you to listen to me."

"What are you doing here?"

"It's over. Put the gun down."

He fought to process Jace's words, just like he'd done on that ridge. The memories continued to filter through his mind. He hadn't been able to answer Jace then, and he couldn't answer him now.

Gunshot to the chest.

Need to get him stabilized.

Get me a unit of plasma.

And then. . .nothing. No memories until he woke up forty-eight hours later.

He'd survived the grid going down.

Kat had not.

Maybe it had been a miracle, but if that were true, then why had God saved him and not Kat?

Garrett shook his head. "He deserves worse than the salt mines for everything he's done. Don't you see, Jace? It wasn't just shooting me. I've seen the list of his crimes."

"That isn't our call, Dad."

Garret's finger brushed the trigger. "They told me they had you."

"They lied. I managed to escape then saw you headed this way. Figured you might need backup, so I circled around."

"You shot him."

"I stopped him, but he'll live."

"He doesn't deserve to live," Garrett argued. "He needs to pay for his crimes."

"Dad, I need you to listen to me."

Garret ignored Jace as he stared into Elijah's eyes and saw fear for the first time. No. He wasn't going to listen to Jace, or anyone for that matter. It was time he got his revenge.

"You can't kill me, McQuaid." Elijah's lip quivered as he begged for his life. "Your son's right. You can't be my judge and jury."

Garrett didn't move. There was something powerful about being able to control someone he hated so much. Of having the control of life and death in his hands. All he needed to do was pull the trigger. God would forgive him. The man deserved the hell that he'd gone through.

As much as you fight it, He's still right here.

The uninvited replay of Margaret's words made him pause. He wanted to scream as the inward battle raged. All he had to do was pull the trigger and this would be over.

But would it?

A burning sensation spread through his finger and up his arm. He took a step back and took his finger off the trigger, unable to stamp out Margaret's voice.

He flipped on the safety and handed Jace the gun. "I need to go."

Nothing had changed. He still wanted the man dead, but he'd fought too long doing the right thing to simply throw it all away now.

"Dad, wait. . ." Jace touched his arm. "Where are you going?"

"Does it matter?" He started to walk away then turned back. "Hope was right. I shouldn't have come. I almost killed a man for revenge. I never thought I'd do something like that."

"But you didn't, and it's over."

"Is it?" Garrett took one last look at Elijah. "I'm just as corruptible as they are."

"You're human, Dad. That's all."

"You don't need me anymore. You never have. You and your siblings, Chase and Kellan. . .you've all done fine without me."

He pressed his hands against his temples, but as hard as he tried, he couldn't suppress the pain. Couldn't push away the searing loss that had torn his heart in two.

"Dad. . .you know that's not true."

Garrett barely heard his son's words as he strode away from the cabin through the thick covering of trees, mounted his horse, then rode away.

CHAPTER FIFTEEN

Morgan kept her sidearm aimed at Adam Duke as her husband helped secure the men who'd threatened to kill them. The men had told them they still had Jace, but obviously that was a lie. She'd lost a lot of people she'd loved, including her first husband. Realizing how close she'd come to going through that again terrified her.

"This isn't over," Elijah said, trying to pull on his binds.

"Oh really?" Jace said, reinforcing Elijah's brother's zip tie with a length of rope. No one was taking any chances of these men getting away. "I don't think you're really in a position to try and threaten us."

Elijah laughed, as if he thought this was some kind of game. "You don't think we've been able to stay under the radar for this long without plenty of resources. People who owe us favors. It's just a matter of time before we're free again."

"Make sure they don't move," Jace said to Kellan and Chase before stepping back and turning to Morgan.

He took her hand, pulled her away from the men, then

drew her tightly against him. "What are you doing out here?"

"I needed to find you." She was sobbing as he held her, caught up in the emotion of just minutes ago not knowing what the men had done to him. "I couldn't lose you."

"You didn't lose me, Morgan. You're not going to lose me."

"You can't promise me that." She looked up at him, her eyes filled with tears. "Tell me what happened. We found blood on the trail, Jace. And a snagged piece of your shirt. I thought you were dead."

"I managed to escape from the cabin."

"And the blood?" She ran her hands down his sleeves, stopping when she found the rip just above his elbow, caked with dried blood.

"I must have snagged it on something. I honestly didn't even know it." He caught her gaze. "I'm fine, Morgan. I promise. What about Noah. Is he okay?"

She nodded. "He's with Tess and Hope."

"I'm so sorry you had to go through all of this. Both of you."

"We'll be fine." She pressed her hands against his chest. "But you need to go after your father."

"I know."

She took a step back. "He's so broken, and seeing the Duke brothers again. . . I'm worried about him."

"I'll be able to track him as long as I leave now and find him before dark. It's starting to snow again."

She blinked back the tears, not wanting to let him out of her sight after finding him again. Tired of the constant danger he was forced to put himself in because of his job. But protecting his family and the town was not just a job for him. It was who he was. And one of the things she loved about him.

"I hate to break up this reunion," Chase said, walking up to them, "but we're going to need to make some decisions. It's going to be dark soon, and I'm not going to be able to relax until these prisoners are locked up, and we find your father."

"Agreed." Jace turned to his brother-in-law then paused. "What happened to you?"

"He was shot back on the train," Kellan said.

Morgan studied Chase's side. "You're bleeding again."

"I'm fine." Chase shook off the concern. "We need to go. My wife can patch me up again once we're home."

Jace hesitated then nodded. "You can take one of the jeeps and transport both the supplies and the prisoners back to town. Morgan, if you can drive, Kellan and Chase can escort you on their horses and make sure you get back safely. I'll take your horse to go after my father."

"Sounds like a solid plan," Kellan said.

Jace turned to her. "Are you sure you're okay with driving?"

She nodded. "I'm more worried about you."

"I'll be fine." He kissed her long and hard before pulling away. "All this is almost over."

"I found the keys," Kellan said, handing them to her.

She pressed the keys against the palm of her hand before sliding into the driver's seat while the men secured their prisoners in the back of the open vehicle.

Jace tapped on the hood of the vehicle. "Kellan and Chase, I'm trusting you to make sure nothing happens to my wife. And if they try anything—and I mean anything—shoot them."

CHAPTER SIXTEEN

Hope fought to control her anxiety as she and Ava rode toward town. Knowing the urgency of Ava's request, it hadn't taken her long to change into dry, warm clothes, grab her medical bag, and get her horse ready. The afternoon sun was working hard to warm the open land before nightfall, but dark clouds in the distance were moving in.

"I don't know about you, but I can almost forget everything that's going on when I'm out here," Hope said. "It's so open. So beautiful."

"Yes, it is."

And it was something she didn't take enough time to enjoy. The beauty was striking in this tucked-away region off the interstate. Most days boasted blue skies along with a night sky that was so clear at times she was certain she could actually touch the stars if she tried.

But as much as she loved it here, it was their isolation that made things more difficult. Shadow Ridge was one of many small and isolated towns across this area of West Texas. After the grid went down, there were towns that had simply disappeared. Which was one of the reasons why letting go of the anxiety wasn't easy. The stress put on her as the only doctor in the area had been difficult.

"How long has Josie been sick?" Hope asked as they left the ranch land and headed down the road toward town. Even the beauty of the afternoon wasn't enough to sidetrack her thoughts for long.

"She was sick a few weeks ago but shook it pretty quickly. She never really complained."

"And this time?" Hope asked.

"A week, maybe a bit longer, but she hasn't been able to get over whatever it is."

"Why didn't you bring her in to the clinic?" Hope asked.

"I probably should have, but I just kept thinking she'd bounce back. She's always been so resilient. And after all she's been through. . ."

Ava didn't have to explain. For a long time, the rift between the sisters had been so deep that Ava almost lost Josie. There had always been a constant trail of drugs and girls crossing through this isolated part of the state. The grid going down hadn't changed anything. Traffickers were still targeting the vulnerable and moving them to places it was impossible for them to get help. Josie had gotten caught up in the web and in the process almost lost everything.

With time had come healing. Josie made some friends —like Tess—and had gotten involved in the community. She and Tess had used notes from Josie's father's journeys as a resource for a water purification system that they'd successfully implemented, making a huge impact on the health of hundreds of people in Shadow Ridge.

"She's come so far and has been doing so well," Ava said, breaking into Hope's thoughts. "I didn't want to have to bring you in on this, but she's just not getting better."

"You know I'm always available for you," Hope said.

Hope breathed in the familiar scent of smoke from cooking fires dotting the terrain as they approached Ava and Levi's house where they lived with Ava's sister Josie. No electricity meant cooking over outdoor fire pits or wood stoves. Some people had built rocket stoves that were hot enough to boil water or cook a basic meal. The temperature had dropped over the past few weeks, a relief from the long hot summer, but now they were facing a long, cold winter without knowing if or when the heating would come back on.

After two cold winters, she knew what would happen.

Without heating or air-conditioning, there was always a spike in mortality. In the summers she'd dealt with heat-related illnesses. In the winter, it was things like hypothermia and influenza.

"Any news from Levi?" Hope asked, needing to keep her mind focused.

"No, but he should be back in the next couple days. What about Chase? Is he home yet?"

Hope hesitated. "He got in last night."

"With the supplies you needed?"

"No," she said as she dismounted from her horse outside Ava's house. "The train was hijacked and the medicines stolen."

"Oh, Hope. . ." Ava pressed her hand against her mouth. "I heard about the hijacking, but I didn't know Chase was on the train."

Hope gave Ava a quick rundown of everything she

knew from the last twenty-four hours then paused. "Morgan went with them."

"I never would have brought you into town knowing you were waiting for your husband."

Hope shook her head. "It's fine. We're family now."

Inside the house, they went down the hall to where Josie was lying down in a room with pink and orange décor out of the seventies.

"Hey," Hope said, stepping into the room. "I heard you've been under the weather."

Josie sat up in the bed and rested her head on the pillow behind her. "I didn't want Ava to bother you. I know you're busy."

"I'm never too busy for you."

"Thank you," Josie said. "And just for the record, once Amazon is making deliveries again, I'm going for a new theme for my bedroom."

"I don't know," Hope said, looking around the room. "I kind of dig the lava lamp, daisy patterns, and dream catchers."

Hope smiled at the young woman, but didn't miss the perspiration that smelled like wet hay as she set down her medical bag.

One of the signs of the infection.

"Tell me what you're feeling," she said.

Josie glanced at her sister, who was still standing in the doorway. "Headache, fever, tired all the time."

"What about muscle pain?"

"Yes. Some vomiting and abdominal pain, but not like cramps." Josie crossed her legs. "Do you know what it is?"

"I might," Hope said. "There is something that's been

going around. It's like the issue we had with the tainted drinking water, except it's with dairy products."

"So you think it's something I ate," Josie said as Hope started listening to her heart.

"If it's what I think it is, the infection is transmitted from animals to humans, typically from unpasteurized milk or other dairy products. It can even come from undercooked meat."

"Wouldn't I be affected as well?" Ava asked, stepping closer to the bed. "I'm not showing any symptoms, and we eat pretty much the same thing."

"People respond differently to the infection, and it's always possible that you didn't eat what Josie did. Maybe she got it at a friend's house."

Josie shrugged. "It's possible."

"I'm gonna need you to make of list of everything you've eaten over the past couple of weeks. Be as detailed as you can."

"Okay."

"I'm waiting to get the antibiotics that we need to treat it, so in the meantime I'm going to give you a compound of herbs I have to help with the symptoms."

"What if they don't get the medicine?" Ava asked as soon as they were back in the living room.

"Thankfully, my husband is a very persistent man, but if he doesn't get it, then we'll go to plan B."

"Which is?" Ava asked.

Hope paused. "Honestly, I don't know yet."

"Then tell me how serious this is."

"There are risks, but Josie is young and in good health." Hope frowned, hating that she didn't have all the answers. "She's not the only one. I've seen these same symptoms in almost a dozen people. She should be fine. Long term, if left untreated, it can affect the heart, or other organs," she said, wanting to be honest, "but Chase should be here soon with the antibiotics."

"She's been doing so well this last year," Ava said, clearly frustrated. "And just when I felt like she's really started healing. . ."

Hope squeezed her hand. "She's going to be okay."

Because she had to be.

"What about you?" Ava asked. "Are you getting the rest you need? You look tired."

"I'll be fine," she said, hoping she sounded better than she felt. "It's been a long day."

"Thank you for coming."

"Of course. And next time don't wait so long. We're family. I'm always here for you."

Hope glanced back at Ava's house as she headed to the ranch. How she was feeling wasn't the only thing she was keeping from Ava. There was something else she hadn't told her. She'd heard the same telling whooshing sound in Josie's heart that she'd heard in Margaret's.

CHAPTER SEVENTEEN

Hope rode back toward the ranch on her mare, fighting the urge to gallop across the frozen landscape. The realization that a child was growing within her, totally dependent on her, had changed everything. And brought out fiercely protective motherly instincts to protect her unborn offspring.

What if I can't protect our child?

The snow had stopped falling, and the sun was out, but an icy wind still whipped through her collar. The white silhouette of the old chapel built from rock and adobe came into view as she headed toward the ranch. Without thinking, she rode up to the chapel, secured her horse, and then slipped through the wooded doors of the quiet structure where they attended church each week.

"Paster Matthew?" She glanced toward the front of the simple sanctuary where the minister was sweeping. "I'm sorry. If I'm interrupting."

"Not at all, Hope," he said, setting the broom down. "This is a good time, actually. I was just doing a bit of cleaning. Most people are staying close to home now that the temperature has dropped."

"How are you?" she asked, walking down the aisle.

"I'm well, but I think I should be asking you that question."

Hope smiled as she sat down on the front pew, trying to put her thoughts into words. Sunlight filtered through the row of glass windows, but she still felt cold inside.

"It's been a long day," she said finally.

"I heard that Chase and your father left this morning to go after the Duke brothers. I'm guessing that they're not back yet?"

"It's probably too early, but no. Not yet."

"I've been praying for them ever since I heard, though if I'm honest, I pray for them daily."

"Thank you. That means more than you'll ever know."

"But. . ."

Hope smiled. "You have this knack of reading minds."

"I like to think it's the working of the Holy Spirit giving me insight.'

She nodded. "I didn't expect to be here—in this place emotionally right now."

"What do you mean?"

"When I look back over everything that's happened, it's hard to believe what we've all been through. This town has somehow managed to stay alive. Thinking I lost Chase, then finding him again. I've held on to my faith, but there have been so many times when I've been angry. Angry at God, people in the town, myself. . ." She let out a sharp breath. "I know that fatigue plays a big part, but I'm tired of feeling out of control. Of having to deal with so many life and death situations when I don't feel capable."

"And you're feeling that anger again right now," Matthew said.

"I just came from seeing a patient. She's young and facing a possible heart issue because I can't get the medicine I need. And she's not the only one."

"You've carried more than your share of the town's burdens, Hope."

She stared at her clasped hands. "When they took down the Realm, I believed this would finally all be over soon, and yet here we are, still fighting. Still without power. The nonstop crisis has worn me thin."

Maybe it was just hormones, but it was frustrating, dealing with emotions on top of everything else. She was the one the town was counting on to keep them well, and yet once again, she was being thrown into another situation she had no control over.

"I'm tired of asking God why, then feeling guilty," she continued. "Trusting Him and then getting hit in the face with another round of doubts."

"It feels like a never-ending problem, doesn't it?" Matthew caught her gaze. "We can look back and see where He's already worked. See His faithfulness in Scripture and in our lives, and yet we still somehow don't take Him at his word." He paused. "It's called the human condition."

Hope couldn't help but grin. "Does that translate into impossible?"

"I guess I have to say yes, because if it weren't true, then that would mean we didn't need Him. And it's why I find myself constantly having to take my thoughts captive, reminding myself of specific times of His faithfulness, along with His miracles in my own life. Every. Single. Day."

Hope let out a sharp breath. The list of God's miracles was long. Even with all the tragedy they faced, she'd still seen God's faithfulness over and over and over. Holding on to that shouldn't be so hard.

But somehow it was.

"Maybe you're asking the wrong question," Matthew said, interrupting her thoughts.

She looked up and caught his gaze. "What do you mean?"

"We tend to ask God why He lets things happen, and yet we might never get the answer to that. We live in a fallen world where things go wrong, people die, and we don't always know why, and yet Jesus told us that in this world we would have troubles."

Hope squeezed her hands together. "Then what am I supposed to ask instead?"

"I've started asking God how I should respond, because the older I get, the more I see that He uses hardships to draw me closer to Him." Matthew looked away. "I'll confess something. Before the grid went down, I was planning to quit."

"Really?"

He nodded. "I was tired of the small numbers every week, of having to ask people to give, of never having enough volunteers. When the grid went down, everything changed. There wasn't money to give, and even if people had money, it wasn't worth anything. Then slowly, people I hadn't seen for years suddenly showed up. They were searching for answers. The same ones you're looking for."

"Sounds like an answer to prayer," she said.

"I've learned that the enemy wants you to get so discouraged that you believe God has forgotten you. In fact," Matthew continued, "he will do whatever it takes to keep us from knowing and following Christ. He might use physical illness, anger, bitterness, doubts, and jealousy. . .anything that causes us to take our focus off Christ and turn us away from our Creator."

"It's still not easy," she said.

"Not at all. Remember how after the grid went down, the city council came together and decided to use a large, empty warehouse on the edge of town to store food for the community?"

Hope nodded.

"I think it was at that moment when I realized that God could redeem this situation."

She tried to analyze his words. Maybe she *was* asking the wrong questions. She'd been challenged by hardship, but in the end, maybe it was her response that was wrong.

"It's called being human, Hope. And as much as the town relies on you, you're only human as well."

She grinned. "I know."

"You think I'm kidding, but I'm serious. It's why Jesus spent time with the Father and why we have to continually renew our minds in the Word. It's not a one-time thing and then we're set for life. It's why we need community, encouragement, and time in the Bible."

"I know you're right. It's just hard sometimes to look beyond my circumstances."

"No, it isn't easy."

"Not when there's an infectious disease I'm trying to fight. My father's struggling, and he and Chase are going after the Duke brothers. . ." She touched her stomach. "I'm so afraid of losing him again."

"Does Chase know?"

She glanced down at her hand, surprised at his perception.

"Not yet."

"You're afraid you could get sick as well," Matthew said.

"Brucellosis is contagious."

"You're carrying a lot right now, and have for a long time. Hebrews chapter ten tells us to hold tightly to our hope. I think God knows that sometimes that means holding on for dear life when we feel like we're about to lose it all."

She looked up from the pew and realized that the sunlight was dimming inside the chapel and darkness would follow soon. "I need to get back to the ranch before dark, but thank you."

"I'm always here."

"I know. And I appreciate it. You've done a lot for this community." Hope stood up. "Know that it's not overlooked. Glad you didn't give up that day."

"Me too."

Hope headed back to the ranch, grateful for the push to change the trajectory of her mindset, but still unable to completely shake the worry. In so many ways her confidence as a doctor had grown the past two years. It seemed ironic that taking over for Dr. Goodman had not only brought her back to her small hometown, but had also thrust her into the middle of a situation she'd never imagined having to deal with. Never imagined she would have the strength to deal with. Maybe Matthew was right and none of this was in vain after all. Maybe God would find a way to redeem this situation.

The lights of a vehicle in the driveway of the ranch

house pulled Hope out of her thoughts, flipping on a warning switch. Undrivable cars were scattered across the county, as they'd run out of fuel months ago. She slowed her horse down, dismounted, and then withdrew her sidearm from the holster before approaching the house and the running motor.

"Hope?"

She heard her husband call her name and let out a lungful of air as she ran toward the veranda where he stood with Jace, Kellan, Tess, and Morgan.

"I'm so glad you're all back." Hope threw her arms around her husband's neck. "Are you okay?"

"I might need a bit of patching up again," Chase said, pulling her against him, "but yes. I'm fine."

"We found them," Jace said. "The Duke brothers are in lockup in town, and we just finished unloading the medicine."

"Margaret and my other patients will be so relieved. I'll be able to get them on a treatment plan right away. . ." Hope looked for her father. "Where's Dad? In with Margaret?"

"No." Jace pulled Morgan tighter against him on the top stair. "We don't know where he is."

"What do you mean you don't know?" she asked.

"He rode off after we took down the Duke brothers. I tried to follow him but lost his tracks up on the ridge. I don't think he wanted to be found."

"You were right," Chase said, catching her gaze. "He never should have gone after the Duke brothers with us."

CHAPTER EIGHTEEN

GARRETT RODE his horse hard across the frozen ground. An icy wind whipped through him, but he barely felt the cold. Instead, it was the anger pressing against his chest that made it hard to breathe. It had been so long since he'd allowed himself to feel. So long since he'd allowed that thirst for revenge to surface. A thin limb snapped against his face as he passed too close to a row of trees, but instead of slowing down, he just shifted his course and kept riding, urging his horse to go faster. And praying that he could somehow find a way to outrun the pain.

Because as hard as he'd tried, the grief he'd taken on after Kat's death had never completely disappeared. The only way he'd even been able to handle it was to ignore it. He hadn't talked to anyone about the simmering emotions because he'd never believed it would help. Even church on Sundays had become a reminder of how far offtrack he'd gotten with his anger. He might be able to say the right words, but loss had left him feeling out of control, birthing the desire for revenge.

He rode through the stretch of open grassland, wishing God would intervene. He'd finally gotten the opportunity he'd been waiting for. He could have shot Elijah right then and there, and in his own mind he would have been justified.

If Jace and the others hadn't been there, he knew what he would've done. He would have pulled that trigger and walked away. His lungs burned in the frigid air. Was that really who he'd become? He'd always been a man who sought to implement justice, not revenge. And yet at that moment, all he had seen was a chance to put an end to the man's life who had taken so much from him.

That was not who he used to be.

That wasn't who he wanted to be.

Getting closer to a grove of pecan trees, he pulled back slightly on the reins, finally urging his horse to slow down. As soon as he came to a stop, he dismounted. What had happened to him? He laced his fingers behind his head and started pacing the snow-crusted ground, trying to catch his breath. Kat would have been so disappointed in him and would've been the first one to talk sense into him. She would have told him that what he was doing was wrong, allowing his entire life to be wrapped up in revenge. Shooting Elijah would do nothing to erase the past two years, nor would it bring back Kat.

Nothing would.

Not even revenge against those who brought down the grid in the first place, causing her death.

The need for justice and revenge screamed inside of him along with the anger and pain.

All it had taken was a group with evil intent to bring down the critical infrastructures. The electric grid, water, transportation networks... That one act of sabotage had taken Kat's life, and nothing he could do or think could change that.

Deep furrows of pain surfaced. No one from the Realm would ever be able to fully understand his loss, but there were thousands who had been affected. Everyone had lost someone.

He was no exception.

And why did he think he was any different?

He walked up to one of the trees and braced his hands against the scaly bark, wanting to scream out to a God who hadn't heard him for the past two years. For all the things that were unfair in all of this. For the things a good God could have stopped.

He started pounding his fists against the tree trunk, stopping only when a trail of blood ran down his knuckles. He wiped the red stain on his pants then took a step back. Minus a slight limp, his health had been restored. All his kids were safe, and except for Sam, were back in Shadow Ridge. Wasn't God behind those blessings? The sudden shift in his thoughts surprised him. He'd gotten so used to dwelling on the anger and frustration, that the negative things had completely overshadowed anything good.

His thoughts shifted again to his children. Despite all of the problems and losses they'd experienced, they'd stood up to the challenge, something he'd always tried to teach them to do.

Something he'd failed to do.

A layer of anger evaporated, replaced by a familiar, dark sadness. He knew his kids worried about him, but for so long he'd lost the desire to care. Even when he'd started walking again and Jace had managed to talk him into working, he'd felt caught in a world where he didn't belong. A reality where he was out of control and lost.

He stared up at the darkening sky and yelled out to God. "What am I supposed to do?"

Nothing.

"Are you even listening?"

This time he was answered by a thunderbolt lighting up the horizon. Proof of God's power? Maybe, but why couldn't a creator God come to him with answers?

His jaw tensed as he watched the light display along the horizon. He never would have imagined grief could last this long, at least not at the soul-searing level he felt it. He'd heard Hope once talk about grief fatigue, and how the grid going down had compounded people's losses. Instead of stopping to mourn for the people they'd loved and lost, they'd all been thrust into survival mode. And it wasn't only friends and family who were gone. They'd lost their entire way of life, and for him, his health and career as well. So instead of grieving when the grid went down, they'd been forced to focus all their energy on survival.

He knew that for himself, his mind was on constant overdrive, and the lingering pain from the bullet along with insomnia meant he was exhausted every day. There were so many triggers that took him by surprise. It was a complicated grief that instead of becoming more manageable as time passed had debilitated him.

His thoughts moved toward Margaret as he sat down on the hard ground and leaned his head against his hands. Grief and loss weren't the only feelings he was battling with. There was also guilt. She'd reached out to him back at the ranch house last night, and he'd brushed her off.

Pushed her away, just as he'd been doing for the past few weeks.

He'd never meant to develop feelings for her, and yet somehow, no matter how hard he fought it, he had. She'd been an oasis in the middle of his emotional desert. Someone who put up with all his anger and frustration and had simply been there for him.

But Margaret had suffered in this as well, and as their growing attraction had terrified him, he'd found himself running away from her and the relationship he knew she wanted.

A relationship he wanted as well, if he were completely honest with himself.

None of this was her fault, but how was he supposed to let her in? She deserved better than him. Someone who wasn't so stubborn and completely buried in the past.

There had been a period of time when he'd let himself pursue her. When he'd actually been able to imagine what it might be to have someone in his life again. But the closer he got to that decision the more fear he felt. So in his mind, he'd come up with a thousand excuses why he couldn't love her. He'd convinced himself that he'd resent her, or end up always comparing her to Kat, which wouldn't be fair to her. How his loneliness wasn't a reason for a relationship.

If he were honest with himself, Margaret's illness had somehow become the final straw as the fear of losing someone he loved again terrified him. So he'd backed off, spending more time in town than out at the ranch. Missing lunch dates with her, and making sure that when they were together, their conversations always steered away from anything personal.

In the process, he knew he'd hurt and confused her, but where did that leave him? He honestly had no idea, but he did know one thing. He didn't like the man he'd become. A man who was hardened, and at the same time ruled by emotion and consumed with fear and anger.

The sound of barking shifted his attention. Ranger ran up to him.

"Ranger." He rubbed the back of the German shepherd's neck. "What are you doing out here, boy?"

Ranger nuzzled his nose against Garrett's face.

"How in the world did you find me?"

His loyal companion just lay down beside him, content to sit with him in the middle of the grief. He felt the dam wall around his heart begin to break. Tears streamed down his face, and this time, he didn't even try to fight the inundation of emotion.

I don't know what to do, God. I don't know how to move on.

There were still no obvious answers in the next thunderbolt that lit up the horizon, but one thing he did know. Until he found a way to let go of his pain, he'd never be able to move on.

CHAPTER NINETEEN

It was dark when Garrett rode up to the house with Ranger just before dawn with nothing more than the moonlight to guide them. He knew these grasslands and mountainous areas well. Better, perhaps, than he knew his own heart.

He quickly settled his horse in the barn then called for Ranger to come with him to the house.

"Dad. . ." Hope jumped up from one of the wooden rockers on the veranda, ran down the steps, and threw her arms around his neck.

"What are you doing up?"

She shook her head. "Waiting for you. I was worried when you didn't return with Chase."

His feet crunched in the snow as he took a step back. "Is everyone safe?"

Hope nodded. "They're all here, while the Duke brothers and their friend are locked up in town and will be getting their sentencing from the judge next time he comes through town."

Garrett nodded. The system was far from perfect, but the setup had worked well over the past year. The fact that those men were about to pay their dues for all the crimes they'd committed relieved him, but it also made him angry that he'd let his hate fester for so long.

"And you have the medicine now?" he asked.

"I've given Margaret her first dose," she said, "and will be giving out the rest tomorrow in town. You don't know what a blessing it is."

"I think I do." He glanced past her. "How is she doing?"

"It's going to take time for her to heal because the bacteria itself incubates within the cells. But now that we have the medicine, I believe we can expect a full recovery for everyone infected. And thankfully, they were able to get the injections, which should work more effectively than the oral drug."

He let out a sharp breath of relief. "Can it come back?"

"It's possible, especially since we don't know yet what the source is, but the treatment is effective. If all things go according to plan, she should be fine in a few weeks."

"I'm relieved to hear that."

"You can go see her. I'll get you some coffee and something to eat—"

"I will, but first. . . Can we walk before we go inside? I need to talk to you."

"Of course." Hope looked back at the house and nodded at Chase, who now stood in the doorway.

Hope took his arm as they started walking, while Ranger kept up next to them.

"Are you warm enough?" he asked.

"I'm fine," she said, pulling her thick poncho closer round her shoulders.

He'd always felt close to his kids, but for some reason Hope was the one he felt he'd disappointed the most.

"I guess Chase told you what happened with the Duke brothers," he said after a couple minutes of silence passed between them. "Why I didn't come back."

"He's been worried, we all have, but he didn't give any details. He said that was up to you."

Another wave of guilt washed through him, almost making him change his mind and not tell her what had happened. He kept walking, waiting for his nerves to calm.

"There was a moment, when Elijah was down and I was standing over him," he finally said. "A moment when I almost pulled the trigger."

He paused again, waiting for his words to sink in.

"But you didn't," she said.

"No. If I had done that, I would have been no different from them." He shook his head. "What I did was almost let my anger, hurt, and revenge put me in a place where I was out of control. I didn't know just how easy it was to get to that place where everything seems so dark, you don't care what you do or about the consequences. I've let pain and anger and hate fester for far too long."

Hope stopped and turned to him. "Dad, tracking those men down, the men who almost took your life couldn't have been easy."

"It wasn't. I spent the night wrestling with God and realizing that I've wasted the past two years."

"No. You lost a lot, Dad. It's okay to take time to grieve."

"I understand that, but there are so many things I

regret in the process. People I've hurt. When I lost your mother and my career, my health... I gave up on everyone. Everything."

"You don't have to apologize."

"But I do, because I'm not the only one who has had to face the traumas they went through. I don't think I've even thanked you for saving my life that day."

Hope reached out and squeezed his hand. "You do know that you were and always will be my favorite patient."

He stopped and turned to her. "And your mother? I haven't forgotten that you were one of the first ones who had to deal with her accident...her dying. Being a first responder can mess with your mind, and when it's a loved one... You had to deal with both of us that weekend. I just...I've never been able to talk about that day."

Her smile faded, and he knew he'd hit a nerve.

"I've never really talked about it to anyone other than to Chase," she said, looking away.

"I know I haven't dealt with all the trauma and grief of those first few months. I've always been a person who just dealt with whatever life threw at me. I'd just keep going, but this... This has always seemed too much."

"What do you remember about that day?" she whispered.

"I remember knowing I was going to die. Then seeing the white lights of the clinic flickering above me, until everything went dark. And when I woke up, Jace told me that your mother was gone."

Hope had told him that another couple inches to the left and the bullet would have hit his heart. Instead, she'd been able to repair the damage.

"You watched your mother die," he said as they kept walking. "You had to piece me back together, and at the same time, you thought you'd lost Chase. I know you're strong, but all of that would affect anyone. And then you were suddenly thrust into caring for the entire town with no resources, no one to consult with or share the load. I honestly don't know how you've done it. And I've spent so much time dealing with my own pain that I never stopped to think about yours or your brothers' and sister's."

"I'm still dealing with the loss of Mom and, to be honest, the loss of the life I thought we'd all live."

Garrett searched for a response. "I've been in law enforcement for my entire adult life. I thought I could handle all of this. Instead, I've felt as if I'm going back to that dark place where I didn't think I would ever see the light again. I've pulled away from you. From your brothers. From Margaret. Back to that place where I felt so lost because everything. . .everything was so out of control, all because of fear. Everything still is out of control. I think I'm afraid of loving someone again because I don't know if I can deal with losing someone again."

Hope turned toward him at the end of the drive as the first rays of sunlight appeared. "You really love her, don't you?"

"I do."

"Dad, I want you to know that I would be so happy if you proposed to Margaret. I miss Mom more than I would have imagined, but I know this is what she would want for you. She'd want you to be happy."

"Really?"

"What did you think I would say? You know we all love

Margaret. I've been expecting this talk for quite a while. I just didn't realize you were struggling so much."

His shoulders dropped, along with some of the guilt he'd been carrying. "I know I made a huge mistake, pushing Margaret away, but she's not the only one."

"What do you mean?" Hope asked.

"I put you through a lot these last couple years. Especially when I'd given up." He took a step back. "But something clicked for me tonight when I was out there, alone with God."

She was quiet as she waited for him to continue.

"I realized what I was capable of, but I also feel as if I've been given a second chance."

"I understand second chances. And I'm grateful for them in both our lives." Hope smiled up at him. "Mom would want you to be happy again, Daddy."

"I know. I just. . .I didn't think I deserved it. Being bitter and angry seemed easier." He managed a smile. The first smile that felt real in a very long time. "I'm proud of you, Hope McQuaid Beckett. I always have been."

Hope laughed. "Thank you. Now, may I make a couple suggestions?"

"Of course."

"Margaret is worried about you. You've kept her waiting long enough, so if you're ready to move on with your life, I'm pretty sure she's awake, reading."

"Good, because for the first time in a very long time, I think I'm ready."

Garrett hesitated outside Margaret's room. The light from a lantern spilled under the doorway, an indication that she was probably up reading, just like Hope had said. He had no idea what her reaction would be. Anger. Worry. Frustration. All he knew was that he'd failed her.

When he finally found the courage to knock, he waited until she told him to come in, then opened the door. She was seated in the rocking chair by the window.

"Garrett." She dropped the book she was reading onto her lap.

"Couldn't sleep?" he said.

"No. I've been worried about you. Chase said you didn't come back with them."

"I'm fine," he said, sitting down on the edge of the bed across from her. "I had a few things to work out. A lot of things, actually."

She nodded at him to continue, but he still had no idea what she was thinking.

"Margaret, I should have said all these things months ago—should have made things official between you and me —because I'm in love with you."

"Wait. . ." Her jaw dropped slightly at the confession. "Are you proposing?

Garrett clasped his hands, wondering if it was possible for him to feel more awkward. "Maybe."

Margaret tilted her head. "I don't know about you, but where I come from, maybe was never a part of a proposal."

He tried to swallow the lump in his throat. "You're not going to make this easy on me, are you?"

She laughed, but her smile quickly faded. "I think you know how I feel about you, but Kat has always been between us."

He shook his head. "It's not her. If anything, it's just me. She would have had us walking down the aisle months ago if she could communicate with me. No, I'm the stubborn one. The one who's afraid of change." He glanced down at his hands. "The one who's afraid of losing the woman I love. And I'm not talking about Kat this time."

"I don't blame you. it's been a difficult journey. But Garrett... You don't owe me anything. You don't have to feel guilty about pulling away from me."

"You don't understand. I realized tonight that I don't want to keep running. I want you and I to move forward together. Not separately. And as for the proposal..."

"Garrett..."

He got down on the floor on one knee beside her and took her hands. "Yes. I'm proposing to you. You've stuck with me no matter how difficult and stubborn I was. You've made me laugh, listened to me, and made sure I didn't give up. I have no idea what the future holds, but I want to spend it with you. So will you marry me, Margaret Anne Wright?"

This time her smile broadened and didn't fade as she cupped her hands around his face. "Yes, Garrett McQuaid. Yes, I'll marry you."

He leaned in and kissed her, realizing that while the pain and loss was still there, he'd finally stopped running.

CHAPTER TWENTY

Ten days later

Hope looked out the window of her childhood bedroom as the sun began to set, sipping chicory coffee and staring out across the pecan and apple orchards below. She and Chase had stayed here last night to be closer to the ranch and her father's wedding.

Her father's wedding.

The thought made her smile, but as happy as it made her, it was hard to fathom that Katherine McQuaid had already been gone for so long. Losing her mother had been one of the hardest things she'd ever gone through, and yet while her heart still felt the loss, she'd found comfort in her father's journey to finally allow himself to be happy again by finding love with Margaret.

It was one of those bittersweet transitions of life.

She took another sip of her coffee then blew out a deep sigh. Margaret would never take her mom's place, and yet their wedding was allowing all of them to finally find a place of joy in the midst of sorrow. Hadn't the same been true in her own life? Finding Chase had completely changed the trajectory of her life and given her a second chance for love. She rested her hand on her stomach. And now they were married with the little one on the way.

She heard someone in the doorway and turned around. Chase walked in, wearing a pair of jeans and a flannel shirt.

"Hey," he said, crossing the room to where she stood in the yellow glow of the lantern light. "You okay?"

"A bit nostalgic, but yes. I want to show you something." She pulled the locket she'd found earlier out of her dress pocket. "I found this while I was looking through my old jewelry box, searching for a pair of my mom's earrings."

"What is it?" he asked as she set the gold locket and chain in his hand.

"It belonged to my mother. There's a photo of her and her mother on one side, and another of her and me on the other."

Chase opened it then held it up toward the light. "You look so much like her."

The punch in the gut she'd felt this morning when she'd found it hit her again. "She's missed all of our weddings, and she's never going to meet our baby."

Chase wrapped his arm around her. "I know you miss her."

"As happy as I am for my father, I really am missing her today." She looked up at him then took a step back after noticing the dirt on his shirt for the first time. "What have you been doing?"

"Tess and Kellan needed some help. Apparently the chicken egg thief was back, but this time they caught a fox. I helped reinforce the fencing."

"Wow," she said, suddenly grateful she and Tess had

run into a squirrel and not a fox. "That sounds a bit unnerving."

"Kellan's going to let it out away from the house." Chase dropped his hands to his sides. "Tess mentioned something about an earlier encounter while I was gone, but said I'd have to ask you about it."

"That can definitely wait for another day," she said, determined to keep her encounter with the flying squirrel a secret as long as she could. She glanced at the suit on the bed she'd laid out for him. "You need to change."

"We've got time." Her heart fluttered as he kissed her firmly on the lips. "You look beautiful, by the way."

"Thank you," she said, laughing. "But distracting me isn't going to work. We've got less than an hour until the wedding starts."

"I heard your father is taking Margaret up to the cabin for a proper honeymoon," Chase said as he headed over to the bed.

Hope watched him examine the suit. "That reminds me of something I wanted to talk to you about, actually."

His eyes widened. "Your father's honeymoon?"

"Not exactly."

"I'm listening."

"Our honeymoon," she said. "Or shall I say the lack of honeymoon. We've been married six months, and we always talk about getting away. I think it's time we figured out a way to make time for us."

"I might actually have the answer to that one," Chase said, pulling off his T-shirt and replacing it with his dark purple dress shirt.

"Really?" She sat down on the edge of the bed.

"So here's the thing," he said, buttoning up his shirt. "I

haven't had the chance to talk to you about this yet, but while Jace and I were in Dallas, I met a man. His name is Grant Taylor. Graduated from medical school about six months before the grid went down and was never able to do his residency. We talked about the need for more medical personnel in places like Shadow Ridge."

"Interesting."

"I thought so. I suggested that he take a trip out here and see what he thinks about working with you and giving you some relief from all your responsibilities."

"Wow." Hope paused. She wanted to be excited, but there were definite concerns. "That would be fantastic, but I don't know this person. I don't know if I would feel comfortable leaving my patients with him."

Chase stopped dressing to brush his lips across hers. "Even if it meant you and I getting away for a few days?"

She grinned. "I might be able to be convinced."

"He's a friend of a friend, but from everything I've heard, extremely responsible and smart, and he actually grew up in a small town in Arkansas. So he understands the needs of small communities."

"When is he coming?"

"I just got a message from him today. He's planning to come out here for a couple weeks—if you are in agreement—and then the two of you can decide if it could be a doable arrangement."

Hope nodded, realizing suddenly how much she wanted this to work. She was going to have to have help if she was going to raise a family.

He knelt in front of her and laid his hands against her belly. "That's not the only reason I'm thinking about getting away. Things probably aren't going to slow down anytime soon."

"True." She laid her hands on top of his. "Maybe this is our chance, Chase, because we can't let ourselves go back to where we were before all this started. And when we have our own children. . . I want them to know what happened, and how we were challenged to appreciate what was right in front of us."

"I'm certainly not missing what's right in front of me." He smiled up at her. "A beautiful wife, for starters."

Hope laughed. "I'm serious, Chase."

"Oh, I'm serious as well. And I agree with everything you've said."

"Hope. . . Chase. . ." someone shouted from downstairs. "Get down here."

Hope glanced toward the door. "What's going on?"

"I don't know." Chase grabbed her hand and pulled her off the bed. "But we're going to find out."

They found everyone standing out on the veranda just as the sun slipped beneath the horizon in the west. Except for Sam and Rebecca, who were planning to be here for Christmas, all of her family was here. Jace, Morgan, and Noah. Tess and Kellan. Levi, Ava, and Josie. And her father and Margaret, who were about to exchange vows.

"Jace. . .Dad. . .what's going on?"

"The lights are coming back on," Noah said, running up to them. "That means we can have Christmas lights this year."

"What?" Hope searched toward the north where the town lay, and saw the glimmer of a white glow coming from Shadow Ridge.

"They turned them back on," Noah said, jumping up and down next to his parents.

It seemed unreal, but Noah was right.

Chase swung Hope around then shouted, "The lights are coming back on!"

Everyone was talking at once as they watched what they'd waited to see for so long. They'd been told to be patient during the transition in getting the grid back up and running, and that it wouldn't be automatic, but that was fine. They were one step closer to having electricity in their homes, at the clinic, and across the county.

Hope leaned against Chase as they stood on the veranda, her hand on her growing stomach as she watched the lights from town shine brighter as darkness settled in. Life was about to change again, and while it might not always be easy, something told her it was going to be far better than she could imagine.

"As happy as I am about the lights coming back on," her father said, over the excited chatter as he took Margaret's hand and caught her gaze, "the preacher has just arrived, and I can't think of a better way to celebrate the grid coming back on then marrying the woman I love."

I HOPE YOU ENJOYED AFTERMATH, the final installment of the Fallout series. Have you read the entire series? **Click here** to start at the beginning with the prequel that started it all!

From USA Today bestselling author of romantic suspense and medical thrillers, Lisa Harris, comes the prequel to a brand new series.

When Dr. Hope McQuaid stops at the scene of an accident on a lonely west Texas highway, she ends up being used as bargaining chip for two dangerous fugitives with nothing to lose. Officer Chase Beckett intervenes in the hostage situation, but he will have to **risk his own life** to save his high school sweetheart—the one woman he's never been able to forget.

Welcome to Shadow Ridge, where LONGMIRE meets JERICHO.

In today's world, law enforcement agencies across the country rely on forensic tools, DNA testing, and crime labs. **But what if that technology was suddenly no longer available?** No one in the small, west Texas town of Shadow Ridge knows what took down the power grid, or when it's going to be back up, but everyone knows exactly where they were the moment it went down. And now, with no electricity, no internet, and no modern technology, the men and women responsible for keeping the town safe are going to have to **learn how to fight crime all over again.**

FALLOUT SERIES
Prequel: The Last Day
Book 1: Survival
Book 2: Hunted
Book 3: Frequency
Book 4: Deception
Book 5: Shattered
Book 6: Aftermath

AGENTS OF MERCY THRILLERS

*USA Today bestselling and award-winning authors Lisa Harris and Lynne Gentry deliver unforgettable and chilling **medical thrillers**.*

Murder on Flight 91

Ghost Heart *(Carol Award finalist)*

Port of Origin (Christy-award finalist)

Lethal Outbreak

Death Triangle

FALLOUT SERIES

From USA Today Best-selling author Lisa Harris comes an epic new series where the survival of Shadow Ridge depends on learning how to fight crime all over again. *Welcome to Shadow Ridge, where LONGMIRE meets JERICHO.*

The Last Day

Survival

Hunted

Frequency

Deception

Shattered

Aftermath

SHADOW STALKERS

What if your mind can't decipher what are truths and what are lies? And what if the truth is more dangerous than the lies your mind believes?
A gripping psychological thriller.

The Lies We Believe (June 2023)

The Secrets We Keep (2024)

The Enemy Between Us

The Truth We Seek

SOUTHERN CRIMES

Despite conflicts that arise between them, the Hunt family is close knit, and when it comes to fighting injustice, they stick together and do whatever it takes to stop that injustice.

Dangerous Passage *(Christy-Award winner)*

Fatal Exchange

Hidden Agenda

THE NIKKI BOYD FILES

A string of missing girls that has haunted the public and law enforcement for over a decade. And for Nikki Boyd, the search is personal. A CBA Best-selling series.

Vendetta *(Christy-Award finalist)*

Missing

Pursued

Vanishing Point

STAND ALONE NOVELS

A Secret to Die For

Deadly Intentions

The Traitor's Pawn

US MARSHAL SERIES

*The purpose of the US Marshals is to
apprehend the most dangerous fugitives
and assist in high profile investigations.
Because if you run, they will find you.
And US Marshal Madison James is one of the best.*

The Escape

The Chase

The Catch

MISSION HOPE

*Romance and adventure drive this two-book series where a doctor is
forced to race against the clock to expose a modern-day slave trade, and*

with an rebel uprising in play, a refugee camp faces the breakout of a deadly and infectious disease with nowhere to run.

Blood Ransom (Christy Award Finalist)

Blood Covenant (Best Inspirational Suspense Novel from Romantic Times)

LOVE INSPIRED SUSPENSE

Deadly Safari

Desperate Escape

Taken

Stolen Identity

Desert Secrets

Fatal Cover-Up

Deadly Exchange

No Place to Hide

The O'Callaghan Brothers Series

Sheltered by the Solider

Christmas Witness Pursuit

Hostage Rescue

Christmas Up in Flames

HISTORICAL

An Ocean Away

Sweet Revenge

Sign up for Lisa's newsletter and keep up with her latest news and book releases!

ABOUT THE AUTHOR

LISA HARRIS is a USA Today bestselling author, a Christy Award finalist for Blood Ransom, Vendetta and Port of Origin, Christy Award winner for Dangerous Passage, and the winner of the Best Inspirational Suspense Novel for 2011 (Blood Covenant) and 2015 (Vendetta) from Romantic Times. She has fifty plus novels and novellas in print. She and her husband currently live in Texas. Visit her website www.lisaharriswrites.com to learn more.

ACKNOWLEDGMENTS

I hope you have enjoyed this series as much as I have enjoyed writing it. Wow! What a journey! There is so much that goes on behind the scene to get my books into my readers hands, and I could never do it on my own. My amazing editor Ellen Tarver. Amanda Geaney for stepping in as my VA and bringing order and help to all my multi-tasking. You're amazing. My sweet husband whose support is never ending, along with his ability to make me laugh and help me when I'm stuck on a plot issues, and my kids who encourage me on the way. And to you my readers who have come along with me on this journey. Thank you!

Selected Praise for Lisa Harris

"This whirlwind fast-paced chase will please fans of Terri Blackstock." **Publishers Weekly** on *The Chase*

"An excellent thriller with well-drawn characters, and the suspenseful start to Harris' new U.S. Marshals series, this will please fans of Catherine Coulter and J. T. Ellison's Brit in the FBI series." **Booklist** on *The Escape*

"Lisa Harris never fails to bring an action-packed, adrenaline-filled romantic suspense to her readers." **Interviews & Reviews** on *The Escape*

"The Traitor's Pawn by Lisa Harris is full of action, mystery, and suspense. From the first page to the last, Lisa Harris captured my full attention." **Urban Lit Magazine** on *The Traitor's Pawn*

"Lisa Harris has quickly become one of my favorite romantic suspense writers." **Radiant Lit Blog** on *Missing*

"An exciting, well-crafted tale of romantic suspense from veteran thriller-writer Harris." **Booklist** on *A Secret to Die For*

Award-winning romantic suspense from the heart of Africa!

BLOOD RANSOM: SNEAK PEEK

PROLOGUE

a narrow shaft of sunlight broke through the thick canopy of leaves above Joseph Komboli's short frame and pierced through to the layers of vines that crawled along the forest floor. He trudged past a spiny tree trunk—one of hundreds whose flat crowns reached toward the heavens before disappearing into the cloudless African sky—and smiled as the familiar hum of the forest welcomed him home.

A trickle of moisture dripped down the back of his neck, and he reached up to brush it away, then flicked at a mosquito. The musty smell of rotting leaves and sweet flowers encircled him, a sharp contrast to the stale exhaust fumes of the capital's countless taxis or the stench of hundreds of humans pressed together on the dilapidated cargo boat he'd left at the edge of the river this morning.

Another flying insect buzzed in his ears, its insistent drone drowned out only by the birds chattering in the treetops. He slapped the insect away and dug into the pocket of his worn trousers for a handful of fire-roasted peanuts, still managing to balance the bag that rested atop his head. His mother's sister had packed it for him, ensuring that the journey—by taxi, boat, and now foot—wouldn't leave his belly empty. Once, not too long ago, he had believed no one living in the mountain forests surrounding his village, or perhaps even in all of Africa, could cook *goza* and fish sauce like his mother. But now, having ventured from the dense and sheltering rainforest, he knew she was only one of thousands of women who tirelessly pounded cassava and prepared the thick stew for their families day after day.

Still, his mouth watered at the thought of his mother's cooking. The capital of Bogama might offer running water and electricity for those willing to forfeit a percentage of their minimal salaries, but even the new shirt and camera his uncle had given him as parting gifts weren't enough to lessen his longings for home.

He wrapped the string of the camera around his wrist and felt his heart swell with pride. No other boy in his village owned such a stunning piece. Not that the camera was a frivolous gift. Not at all. His uncle called it an investment in the future. In the city lived a never-ending line of men and women willing to pay a few cents for a color photo. When he returned to Bogama for school, he planned to make enough money to send some home to his family—something that guaranteed plenty of meat and cassava for the evening meal.

Anxious to give his little sister, Aina, one of the sweets tucked safely in his pocket and his mother the bag of sugar he carried, Joseph quickened his steps across the red soil, careful to avoid a low limb swaying under the weight of a monkey.

A cry shattered the relative calm of the forest.

Joseph slowed as the familiar noises of the forest faded into the shouts of human voices. More than likely, the village children had finished collecting water from the river and now played a game of chase or soccer with a homemade ball.

The wind blew across his face, sending a chill down his spine as he neared the thinning trees at the edge of the forest. Another scream split the afternoon like a sharpened machete.

Joseph stopped. These were not the sounds of laughter.

Dropping behind the dense covering of the large leaves, Joseph approached the outskirts of the small village, straining his eyes in an effort to decipher the commotion before him. At first glance everything appeared familiar. Two dozen mud huts with thatched roofs greeted him like an old friend. Tendrils of smoke rose from fires beneath rounded cooking pots that held sauce for evening meals. Brightly colored pieces of fabric fluttered in the breeze as freshly laundered clothes soaked up the warmth of the afternoon sun.

His gaze flickered to a figure emerging from behind one of the grass-thatched huts. Black uniform ... rifle pressed against his shoulder ... Joseph felt his lungs constrict. Another soldier emerged, then another, until there were half a dozen shouting orders at the confused villagers who stumbled onto the open area in front of them. Joseph watched as his best friend Mbona tried to fight back, but his hoe was no match against the rifle butt that struck his head. Mbona fell to the ground.

Ghost Soldiers!

A wave of panic, strong as the mighty Congo River rushing through its narrow tributaries, ripped through Joseph's chest. He gasped for breath, his chest heaving as air refused to fill his lungs. The green forest spun. Gripping the sturdy branch of a tree, he managed to suck in a shallow breath.

He'd heard his uncle speak of the rumored Ghost Soldiers—mercenaries who appeared from nowhere and kidnapped human laborers to work as slaves for the mines. Inhabitants of isolated villages could disappear without a trace and no one would ever know.

Except he'd thought such myths weren't true.

The sight of his little sister told him otherwise. His mind fought to grasp what was happening. Blood trickled down the seven-year-old's forehead as she faltered in front of the soldiers with her hands tied behind her.

No!

Unable to restrain himself, Joseph lunged forward but tripped over a knotty vine and fell. A twig snapped, startling a bird into flight above him.

The soldier turned from his sister and stared into the dense foliage. Joseph lay flat against the ground, his hand clasped over the groan escaping his throat. The soldier hesitated a moment longer, then grabbed his sister's arm and pulled her to join the others.

Choking back a sob, Joseph rose to his knees and dug his fingers into the hard earth. What could he do? Nothing. He was no match for these men. If he didn't remain secluded behind the cover of the forest he too would vanish along with his family.

The haunting sounds of screams mingled with

gunshots. His grandfather fell to the ground and Joseph squeezed his eyes shut, blackness enveloping him. It was then, as he pressed his hand against his pounding chest, that he felt the camera swinging against his wrist. He stared at the silver case. Slowly, he pressed the On button.

This time, the world would know.

With a trembling arm Joseph lifted the camera. Careful to stay within the concealing shade of the forest, he snapped a picture without bothering to aim as his uncle had taught him. He took another photo, and another, and another ... until the cries of his people dissipated on the north side of the clearing as the soldiers led those strong enough to work toward the mountains. The rest—those like his grandfather, too old or too weak to work in the mines—lay motionless against the now bloodstained African soil.

In the remaining silence, the voices of two men drifted across the breeze. English words were foreign to his own people's uneducated ears but had become familiar to Joseph. What he heard now brought a second wave of terror ...

"Only four more days until we are in power ... There is no need to worry ... The president will be taken care of ... I can personally guarantee the support of this district ..."

Joseph zoomed in and took a picture of the two men.

A monkey jumped to the tree above him and started chattering. One of the beefy soldiers jerked around, his attention drawn to the edge of the clearing. Joseph froze as his gaze locked with the man's. Someone shouted.

If they caught him now, no one would ever know what had happened to his family.

Joseph scrambled to his feet as the soldier ran toward

him, but the man was faster. The butt of a rifle struck Joseph's head. He faltered, but as a trickle of blood dripped into his eye, he pictured Aina being led away ... his grandfather murdered in cold blood ...

Ignoring the searing pain, Joseph fought to pull loose from his attacker's grip, kicked at the man's shins. The soldier faltered on the uneven terrain. Clambering to his feet, Joseph ran into the cover of the forest. A rifle fired, and the bullet whizzed past his ear, but he kept moving. With the Ghost Soldier in pursuit, Joseph sprinted as fast as he could through the tangled foliage and prayed that the thick jungle would swallow him.

BLOOD RANSOM: CHAPTER ONE

MONDAY, NOVEMBER 16, 3:11 PM

KASILI OUTDOOR MARKET

Natalie Sinclair fingered the blue-and-yellow fabric that hung neatly folded on a wooden rod among dozens of other brightly colored pieces, barely noticing the plump Mama who stood beside her in hopeful anticipation. Instead she gazed out at the shops that lined the winding, narrow paths of the market, forming an intricate maze the size of a football field. The vendors sold everything from vegetables and live animals to piles of secondhand clothing that had been shipped across the ocean from charities in the States.

Natalie stepped across a puddle and turned to glance beneath the wooden overhang at the stream of people passing by. Even with the weekend over, the outdoor market was crowded with shoppers. Hip-hop style music played in the background, lending a festive feel to the sultry day. But she couldn't shake the uneasy feeling in the pit of her stomach.

Someone was following her.

She quickened her steps and searched for anything that looked out of place. A young man weaved his bicycle through the crowded walkway, forcing those on foot to step aside. A little girl wearing a tattered dress clung to the skirt of her mother, who carried a sleeping infant, secured with a length of material, against her back. An old man with thick glasses shuffled past a shop that sold eggs and sugar, then stopped to examine a pile of spark plugs.

Natalie's sandal stuck in a patch of mud, and she wiggled her foot to pull it out. Perhaps the foreboding sensation was nothing more than the upcoming elections that had her on edge. All American citizens had been warned to stay on high alert due to the volatile political situation. Violence was on the rise. Already a number of joint military-police peacekeeping patrols had been deployed onto the streets, and there were rumors of a curfew.

Not that life in the Republic of Dhambizao was ever considered safe by the embassy, but neither was downtown Portland. It was all a matter of perspective.

And leaving wasn't an option. Not with the hepatitis E outbreak spreading from the city into the surrounding villages. Already, three health zones north of the town of Kasili where she lived were threatened with an outbreak. She'd spent the previous two weeks sharing information about the disease's symptoms with the staff of the local government clinics, as well as conducting awareness campaigns to inform the public on the importance of proper hygiene to prevent an epidemic.

In search of candles for tonight's party, Natalie turned sharply to her left and hurried up the muddy path past wooden tables piled high with leafy greens for stew, bright red tomatoes, and fresh fish. Rows of women sat on wooden stools and fanned their wares to discourage the flies that swarmed around the pungent odor of the morning's catch.

Someone bumped into her from behind, and she pulled her bag closer. Petty theft might be a constant concern, but she knew her escalated fears were out of line. Being the only pale foreigner in a sea of ebony-skinned Africans always caused heads to turn, if not for the novelty, then for the hope that she'd toss them one or two extra coins for their supper.

Her cell phone jingled in her pocket, and she reached to answer it.

"When are you coming back to the office?" Stephen's to-the-point greeting was predictable.

"I'm not. I'm throwing a birthday party for you tonight, remember? You let me off early." A pile of taper candles caught her eye in a shop across the path, and she skirted the edge of a puddle that, thanks to the runoff, was rapidly becoming the size of a small lake.

Stephen groaned. "Patrick's here at the office, and he's asking questions."

She pulled a handful of coins from her pocket to pay for the candles. "Then give him some answers."

"I can't."

Natalie thrust the package the seller had wrapped in newspaper into her bag and frowned. Patrick Seko, the former head of security for the president, now led some sort of specialized task force for the government. Lately, his primary concern seemed to revolve around some demographic research for the Kasili region she'd been compiling for the minister of health, whose office she worked for. Her expertise might be the prevention and control of communicable diseases, but demographics had always interested her. Why her research interested Patrick was a question she'd yet to figure out.

The line crackled. Maybe she'd get out of dealing with Patrick and his insistent questions after all.

"Stephen, you're breaking up."

All she heard was a garbled response. She flipped the phone shut and shoved it back into her pocket. They'd have to finish their conversation at the party.

"Natalie?"

She spun around at the sound of her name. "Rachel, it's good to see you."

Her friend shot her a broad smile. "I'm sorry if I startled you."

Natalie wanted to kick herself for the uncharacteristic agitation that had her looking behind every shadow. "I'm just a bit jumpy today."

"I understand completely." Rachel pushed a handful of thin braids behind her shoulder and smiled. "I think everyone is a bit on edge, even though with the UN's presence the elections are supposed to pass without any major problems. No one has forgotten President Tau's bloody take over."

Natalie had only heard stories from friends about the current president's takeover seventeen years ago. Two elections had taken place since then and were assumed by all to have been rigged. But with increasing pressure from the United States, the European Union, and the African

Union, President Tau had promised a fair election this time no matter the results. And despite random incidences of pre-election violence, even the United Nations was predicting a fair turnover under their supervision—something that, to her mind, remained to be seen.

Natalie took a step back to avoid a group of uniformed students making their way through the market and smiled at her friend. After eighteen months of working together, Rachel had moved back to the capital to take a job with the minister of health, which meant Natalie rarely saw her anymore. Something they both missed. "What are you doing in Kasili?"

"I'm heading back to Bogama tomorrow, but I'm in town because Patrick has been meeting with my parents to work out the *labola*."

"Really? That's wonderful." Her sentiment was genuine, even though she happened to find Patrick overbearing and controlling—as no doubt he would be in deciding on a bride price. She hugged her friend. "When's the wedding ceremony?"

Rachel's white teeth gleamed against her dark skin, but Natalie didn't miss the shadow that crossed her expression. "We're still discussing details with our families, but soon. Very soon."

"Then I'll expect an invitation."

"Of course." Rachel's laugh competed with the buzz of the crowd that filed past them. "And by the way, I don't know if Patrick mentioned it to you, but Stephen invited us to the birthday party you're throwing for him tonight. I hope you don't mind."

"Of course I don't mind." Natalie suppressed a frown. Stephen had invited Patrick to the party? She cleared her throat. "Stephan did just call to tell me Patrick was looking for me, but it had something to do with my demographic reports. Apparently he has more questions."

"Patrick can be a bit ... persistent." Rachel flashed another broad smile, but Natalie caught something else in her eyes she couldn't read. Hesitation? Fear? "I'll tell him to wait until they are compiled. *Then* he can look at them."

Natalie laughed. "Well, you know I'm thrilled you're coming."

She would enjoy catching up with Rachel, and she had already prepared enough food to feed a small army. It was Patrick and his antagonistic political views she dreaded. She'd probably end up spending the whole evening trying to avoid them both.

"I'm looking forward to it as well." Rachel shifted the bag on her shoulder. "But I do need to hurry off. I'm meeting Patrick now. I'll see you tonight."

Natalie watched until her friend disappeared into the crowd, wondering what she'd seen in her friend's gaze. It was probably nothing. Rachel had been right. Her own frayed nerves were simply a reaction of the tension everyone felt. By next week the election would be over and things would be back to normal.

A rooster brushed her legs, and she skirted to the left to avoid stepping on the squawking bird. The owner managed to catch it and mumbled a string of apologies before shoving it back in its cage.

Natalie laughed at the cackling bird, realizing that this was as normal as life was going to get.

Spotting a woman selling spices and baskets of fruit two shops down, she slipped into the tiny stall, determined to enjoy the rest of the day. She had nothing to worry about. Just like the UN predicted, the week would pass without any major incidents. And in the meantime, she had enough on her hands.

She picked up a tiny sack of cloves, held it up to her nose, and took in a deep breath. With the holiday season around the corner, she'd buy some extra. Her mother had sent a care package last week filled with canned pumpkin, chocolate chips, French-fried onions, and marshmallows. This year Natalie planned to invite a few friends over for a real Thanksgiving dinner. Turkey, mashed potatoes, green-bean casserole, pumpkin pie—

Fingers grasped her arm from behind. Natalie screamed and struggled to keep her balance as someone pulled her into the shadows.

Grab your copy here!

Made in the USA
Monee, IL
17 December 2023

49600977R00104